THE GODDESS IS ANGRY

JB TREPAGNIER

The Goddess is Angry Copyright © 2023 JB Trepagnier

Cover by Hannah Sternjakob Designs

Edited by Michelle Hoffman

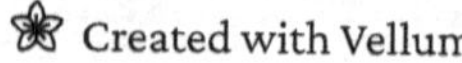 Created with Vellum

THE GODDESS IS AWAKENED

My mom never told me there was a heart-stealing murderer at the Academy of the Profane.

But here we are. I thought I'd be navigating classes, mean girls, and boys. Not this. Never in a million years this. I can't unsee what they did to that witch. And honestly? With the history of this academy, it could be a curse, a ghost, or someone like me doing it.

But I have a team and my twin. And another god on my side. If anyone can stop this, it's us.

THE PROFANE WORLD

THE ACADEMY OF THE PROFANE

GEORGE

It was such a shit show. The Sigmis dorm was trying to figure out why all the Banshees on campus shrieked. Dot, our dorm mother, locked the dorm down and told us to get back to our rooms. She said we could go to each other's rooms, but once we were there, we had to stay put until she counted us.

My dorm room was a nice size, but it wasn't my sister's two girlfriends and my four kinda, maybe boyfriends size. Especially since West was massive and hogging my bed. Mags and Matilda had Mina smashed between them and were snuggling with her because she'd had a bad night.

And West, apparently, figured out my secret and didn't give a shit. It was a giant omen that the Banshees shrieked when I was going to tell them the first time, but I really should. West thought it was cool. I wasn't dating Mina, but I could see the look on my twin's face. Matilda had it bad.

I was about to open my mouth. I swear to shit; I was *literally* about to tell everyone here that I was really a god when a knock interrupted me. Dot stuck her head in with a clipboard. She didn't even blink at all the people in our room.

"You'll all need to stay here. I'm not sure when I'll get the clear for you all to go home. It's probably nothing, but we have to keep you here until we know the campus is safe. If it's a revenant again, we'll send your daddy out. He'll use it as a teaching moment. Professor Morningstar is so dreamy."

Ew. She did not sexualize my dad in front of me. All my dads took my mom's last name when they got handfasted, but Gabriel was already Professor Morningstar and a legend for the whole revenant thing before that. So, he was Gabriel Bell at home and on all his paperwork, but people still called him Gabriel Morningstar. My mom didn't care, so I didn't.

I did care about my dorm mother crushing on my dad because gross.

"It's not nothing. Someone *died*," Ren said.

"I'm not trying to make light of it," Dot said. "One thing you'll learn as students here. No one graduates from this university without hearing the Banshees shriek or shrieking if you're a Banshee like Mina. I've been here for decades. Sometimes, it really is nothing, I promise," Dot said, closing the door to resume her count.

"It's never nothing," Mina said. "If we scream, *someone* is going to die. It's never a false alarm. We can tell if it's violent or not, but it's still sad when someone dies of old age. They have family and people who love them."

"They don't want *us* to know that," Mags said. "Azren is here. I'll bet the board tries to cover this up."

"Going to be pretty hard to do that when everyone heard the Banshees," Church said.

"Azren won't let them," Oscar said. "This is the first time I've seen them outside of history, but if they are really here to stop this, they won't let them."

No, they wouldn't.

"Azren is the headmaster now, and they outrank the board. The board can tell them what to do, but it's going to look *really* bad if they fire a primordial. All Azren has to do is make a big, stinky, bear shifter fart about why they fired them," West said.

"Usually, I punch people in the face for saying shit like that about shifters, but you're also a shifter and you aren't wrong," Matilda said.

"Please don't. I've seen you in magical combat and you're a fucking beast. You've never once broken a nail and your makeup is still perfect when you shift back. If I didn't know better, I'd say you were a hybrid and doing some kind of witchcraft. I'm definitely not fucking with the Hellhound half of the twins," West said.

"I don't think any of us are," Church said.

Church was leaning against my wall and before Matilda could say anything, Bethany rose through the floor and punched him in the dick again. Church shrieked and collapsed on the floor holding his junk. That was enough. Was Bethany seriously in here dick punching my boyfriend after what we just saw on the dodgeball field?

"Seriously, Bethany?" I asked. "I know this is your one night for mayhem, but do you really want to spend it punching my boyfriend in the junk with everything else going on? There's a murderer on campus. You saw what they did to that witch. There are enough ghosts on this campus to get justice for her. Especially on Samhain. You know who did this. You could bring them to Azren to handle."

Everyone who didn't share a crib with me gasped. You just didn't talk to ghosts like that. Church's dick was case in point. They didn't eat, and they didn't sleep. They got all their entertainment from the living. Especially plotting their revenge if you slighted them.

Bethany could out me to this entire room. That wasn't the worst thing that could happen. My secret wasn't more important than the safety of the students here. I didn't think Bethany would do that. The ghosts all had immense respect for gods. That should extend to me, too, even if I wasn't a god of anything and I'd been born and not made.

Bethany just bowed her head.

"Even the pretty death god can't stop him," she said, flying out of the window.

"What does that even mean?" Church groaned.

"Come get in bed and snuggle with me," I said.

I could subtly heal him under the covers, where no one could see my healing light.

"How did you talk to a ghost like that?" Oscar asked. "I speak to them differently, but you can't disrespect them."

"Yes, George. How *did* you talk to Bethany like that?" Mags asked.

I threw a pillow at her face as I climbed into bed behind Church.

"You're little spoon, big boy," I said. "Live it, love it."

"I want to be little spoon," West grumped.

"Dude, we all want to be her little spoon," Ren said.

"Middle spoon is where it's at," Mina sighed.

I was sending a slow, steady stream of healing energy into Church without blasting him and tipping everyone off. I could have told them, but I didn't get interrupted once trying to tell them. It was twice now. I'd have to psych myself up to tell them a third time.

I could hear people in the hall and Dot yelling. Ren stuck his head out and then shut the door.

"We can all go back to our rooms, but we can't leave Sigmis yet."

"Want to come back to my dorm?" Mina asked. "My roommate is obsessed with one of the sirens that was playing at the moon orgy. She's been staying with him most nights. I think he's getting sick of her. It'll just be us."

"Will you be okay?" Matilda asked.

"I'm not a muffin muffler if that's what you're planning on doing. I'll be fine."

"We'll stay with her," Ren said.

"If you mistreat my twin, I'll shift and eat you," Matilda said.

"And my revenge will be epic," Mags said.

Oscar just nodded his head.

"Noted. We want some alone time with your sister. I swear we won't hurt her."

"Unless she asks for it. Then, it's okay," Matilda said, tossing her hair over her shoulder and leaving.

"Do you like a little spanky spank?" Ren smirked.

"I actually don't know," I said thoughtfully.

Did I? We could find out later.

REN

I was learning some important things about myself in college. One was that I was pretty sure I was going to get my third tail any day now. I wasn't the only Kitsune here, but I was definitely the youngest. I had more tails than some of the older Kitsunes.

Foxes weren't pack animals, so they weren't trying to recruit me for the group thing, but there were definitely some Kitsunes here who thought we shouldn't be with anyone who wasn't a Kitsune and kept trying to steal me from Oscar.

The stupid, stuck up Kitsunes were going to lose their shit because I also learned something else about myself. I liked George before. She was cool, and I wasn't opposed to possibly joining her coven. But I just saw a dead body and found out there was a murderer on campus who drew the God of Death here.

And now I was *all* about George Bell and whatever coven she might be forming.

If she just wanted to snuggle, we could do that, but she didn't strike me as a shrinking violet. I could just look at Oscar and tell what he was thinking. We'd known each other that long. Oscar was built to form a coven. I knew that when I kissed him for the first time. He could have made one from just men, but we liked women, too. She just needed to be really impressive.

"Please don't be mad at me, but every time I've tried to tell you my secret tonight, I've gotten interrupted. That has to be a giant-ass sign. I tried again when we got back, but Dot knocked on the door."

Oscar got up and wrapped his arms around her waist. She seemed to think we were going to be mad she wasn't telling us. I was going to have to steal her something big to cheer her up this time.

"I'm a Brujo and Ren is a Kitsune. You don't have to tell us about omens."

Seriously. I might not be a warlock or Brujo, but we believed in omens just as strongly as one. George spun around in Oscar's arms and her eyes got hooded. She was pretty tall, but not as tall as Oscar. George looked up at him through her lashes with those stunning silver eyes.

"You know, you haven't kissed me yet."

If she wanted to do that, we could do that, too. Oscar yanked her to his chest and cocked his head at me. I came up behind her to press myself against her back. Oscar took her mouth. I brushed her hair off of her shoulder and started kissing her neck. She moaned and melted against us.

"Is it wrong that after everything we just saw, I want this?"

"Fuck no. There's a killer on campus. Some people get

hysterical. Other people get horny," I said, nibbling on her ear.

"We can do whatever you want," Oscar said. "It's also okay to be afraid."

I loved Oscar to death, but he did not just say that to George Bell. I watched her on the dodgeball field because I didn't want to look at that dead witch. She wasn't scared. She was hyper-focused on finding out who did this and making them pay. Her dad was a primordial, and her uncle was Loki. We hadn't said anything because she hadn't, but I smelled Azren all over her more than once. I was pretty sure we were all dating a god by extension now.

"Pretty sure George isn't scared of serial killers," I said. "You've seen her in magical combat."

"Distract me," she pleaded. "There's magical lube in my nightstand."

Was she scared? George and Azren appeared to be working on this as a side project. The only reason the rest of us even knew more than a few details she gave us was that we happened to be in her dorm room when the Banshees started shrieking and Azren came to get her.

None of us were mad about that and Azren was transparent, but they were also doing their job on the dodgeball field instead of giving us every detail.

"One question and then we'll be happy to distract you. Is the person doing this targeting witches?"

"No one knows. Bethany won't spill, and we'll know more about how they covered it up in the past with how they try to do it this time. Azren is in a good position to get the details we need while Headmaster Krauss is recovering."

I started giggling. I'm sorry, but the shit that went down with Kaylee and her mom was probably going to be funny until I graduated. I already downloaded the video just in case someone made Dexter take his down so I could watch it again and put it right back up.

Oscar started laughing because Dexter zoomed in on Kaylee and Headmaster Krauss's faces to get a reaction shot when they realized the hex didn't hit George and it was *priceless*. I didn't know what Dexter wanted to be when he grew up, but he shot pretty amazing footage with a cell-phone camera and could do whatever he wanted.

George melted and started laughing with us.

"She was trying to hex me while my back was turned because it's the only way she could beat me. Every witch who saw that video is looking down on her and calling her a coward for not facing me like a true witch. I should be mad about that, but they also pissed off my brother's boyfriend and his revenge was epic."

I couldn't stop laughing because Dexter and her brother were fucking hilarious. Not the fact that they were together. I didn't give a shit about that.

"Your brother is doing the whole growly avenging angel, so no one is mean to Dexter, but I think this whole school is more scared of Dexter than they are your brother," I wheezed. "Dexter *fucked up* the headmaster by uttering one word in a way that absolutely couldn't be blamed on him because he was warning you. Seriously, Headmaster Krauss can't even open her curtains for at least two months without being in excruciating pain. He has the whole freedom of speech thing on his side with the video."

Oscar started laughing.

"That level of fuckery can get a Kitsune a new tail, so Ren has a deep appreciation for it."

Since the academy was warded, people walked around with their wings out if they had them. The Kitsunes half shifted with our ears and we were *all* bragging about our tails. I had two beautiful bushy tails and you can bet your ass I was showing them off.

George gave me a sly look and started stroking my tails. That was highly erotic for us. I couldn't help clicketing in pleasure. Oscar said he missed that noise the most when he lost his hearing. Foxes made it during mating season and Tanuki, my god, decided Kitsunes was going to make it, too.

"Undress me and tell me how you got a second tail so soon."

Stroking my ego *and* my tail? Yes, please. Talking about our tails was a favorite thing, and it meant a lot when someone asked. We took our time stripping her of her clothes, kissing and biting as we removed each article.

"I turned eighteen early, so I had my magic for a few months before graduation. Oscar and I used to hang with our other neighbor, who was a vampire and also turned eighteen early. So, we've got a vampire and Oscar, who nearly went pro at dodgeball, and me, with Kitsune magic and everything that comes with that.

"We filled a metric fuck-ton of balloons with mayonnaise and hung them all over the ceiling. The students ignored them because they had a pretty good idea it was me and my group that did it. The faculty gave the balloons a wide berth because they suspected me, too.

"Our principal was a huge dick. All he cared about was our dodgeball team and he gave the athletes special preference. Oscar was dead to him when he got hurt and I *owed* him. He tried to rip a balloon down and ended up covered in warm mayonnaise.

"Everyone who wasn't an athlete and got bullied by them while he looked the other way jumped into action and started pelting him with mayo balloons. Then the jocks he always coddled got caught up in it and started throwing balloons at him, too. He went home to shower, but the balloons were everywhere. Every time his back was turned, he got hit.

"He looked like he starred in some extreme fetish video about cream pies and the mayonnaise had long spoiled, so you could smell him from across the school. He constantly threw me in detention and was always throwing cheerleaders at Oscar. I gained a tail and the power of telekinesis popping those balloons. I regret nothing."

I really didn't. That man loathed me. He didn't care if the rest of his students were gay or bisexual. He thought dodgeball players were the epitome of manly men and *they* weren't supposed to be bisexual. He thought they were all supposed to be with the cheerleaders. He also just ignored the fact that women had always played dodgeball and some of them were better than the men.

"That was epic," George said.

So was George without her clothes on. Holy shit. She was tall with lean muscles from playing dodgeball. Those legs were perfection. Her breasts were perky, and that ass was super tight. If Oscar and I were going to be with a woman, George was exactly what I pictured.

My boyfriend was polite and respectful, but he turned into a bit of a caveman in the bedroom. He knew how to manhandle me just right. George was an insanely powerful witch with more gods in her family than anyone had met in the past several hundred years, and Oscar totally manhandled her, too.

He picked her up and threw her on the bed. Unless something went down with West and Church, I was pretty sure no one had ever done that to her before, because her dad was probably terrifying. George looked like she was loving every minute and totally not going to tell her dad about this.

I already knew how I wanted to play this, but foreplay first. One thing I was learning about George. She would manhandle us back. Oscar needed that, and I loved it. I dove between her legs, and Oscar pressed his cock against her lips.

I'd seen her in magical combat. She hadn't given off any displays of how strong her magic was aside from giving Kaylee snakes for hair, but I could feel how much power she gave off. She could have flung Oscar across the room for just assuming she wanted to suck his cock, but she didn't. George opened her mouth and grabbed his ass to pull him in deeper.

She was so damned beautiful. I was flicking my tongue on her clit while Oscar fucked her mouth. I slid my fingers inside her and started working her G Spot. George was responsive as hell and she tasted divine. Oscar and I alternated who was in control, but he was never passive when someone was sucking his cock. George had an amazing gag reflex because I'd done this with Oscar countless times before, and it took me a while to control mine with him.

Oscar couldn't hear cries of pleasure anymore, but he could feel them, which is what I had planned later. I doubled my efforts, both to make her feel good and so Oscar could feel her cries around his cock. I learned from her cries and writhing what she liked and kept doing it until she came on my tongue and all over Oscar's cock.

Perfect.

George stretched and looked extremely pleased with herself.

"You two come as a set and I'm not getting between that. You probably have preferences with what you do together that I haven't learned yet. So, teach me how to be a part of you. I have a pretty good idea of how Oscar likes things. How do you want me?

"With Oscar between us," I said.

The first time Oscar and I made love after his accident, we stayed up late talking. We didn't lose anything, but he said he missed hearing the noises I made. So, after that, we experimented with different positions where he could feel me. If he was between George and me, he could feel both of us. I couldn't give him his hearing back, but I could try to give him the little things I could.

George just sighed and stretched like a cat.

"That sounds perfect."

I got the lube out of her nightstand. She got the good kind, too. This is what Oscar and I used. It was functional and got the job done. The first time Oscar and I experimented with a woman, she had glitter lube, for some insane reason. It chafed and my cock looked like a disco ball for a while. Glitter dick really had me doubting I was also into sex with women for a hot minute.

Prepping Oscar was easy. I could do this in my sleep. I knew exactly how he liked it. If Oscar wasn't the passive type in bed, George wasn't either. I knew how Oscar liked to be touched and she was doing it just right. She was licking and biting how he liked it.

When Oscar was ready, he shoved George on her back and she let him. And George took it a step further. She spread her legs and started massaging her clit with hooded eyes. Damn, she looked good. Oscar had Chantico, but he couldn't shift into an animal. He didn't have anything growly built in, but he gave a pretty passable growl when he took her in. So did I, for that matter.

Oscar groaned as he slid into her. I gave them a minute

to get settled, then added a bit more lube to my cock. I lined my cock up with his ass and slowly pressed in. Oscar's ass was divine. Eventually, I'd know what George felt like, too.

George had these insanely long legs. She could stretch them out and hook them behind my ass. Yeah, George wasn't a passive witch. She could have laid there while I fucked Oscar and Oscar fucked her. George totally didn't do that. She was telling me how she wanted it with her heels on my ass.

And I loved every minute of it. I mostly only took directions in bed. If you tried to tell me what to do when I wasn't fucking, I usually reacted badly. But this? George could top me all day, even if she was technically on the bottom right now.

Oscar enjoyed it like this, too. The harder I fucked his ass, the more he pounded into George. Sometimes, we were like this together, but George seemed to really love it, too. It was perfect and neither of us was going to last long at this pace. We were honestly just waiting for George.

I could feel a tingling in my spine that it was going to happen any minute now. We weren't exactly having much sex in the dorms. Church usually went where George was, but West was a little clingy, even though he knew damned well I'd learned sign language as a child because of my sister. I was pent up and wishing we'd done something together before this, so we'd last a little longer.

Oscar had a plan. He wedged his hand between them and started massaging her clit. Oscar always had a plan, even when it came to sex. George was clawing his back and screaming her orgasm shortly. I could finally let go. I stopped holding back and let my orgasm overtake me.

My world exploded as I spilled into Oscar. He wasn't

that far behind me. I knew Oscar's happy noises. His orgasm was just as big as mine.

It was a tight fit, but we were able to squeeze into George's bed to snuggle. I couldn't believe I didn't like her at first. She was perfect for us. Her humor matched ours, and talking to her was easy. George matched us sexually, too.

She was perfect for us. And to think, I almost told her to get lost when she sat down at my table looking for that commission. I was an idiot sometimes.

AZREN

These people were something. There was a time the mortals in this realm respected Death. They revered it and they honored their dead. They honored *me*. I went back to the dodgeball field after I got the students away and the Paranormal Investigation Bureau shooed me away like they were better equipped to handle death than I was.

Bitches.

So, I went and found Fleur's coven. I sat them down and told them what happened without all the brutal details. I promised them I'd get revenge for them.

"I need your help. I spoke to her ghost and helped carry her to the Aether. The dead don't remember their last moments. It's a kindness. She didn't remember going to the dodgeball field. Can any of you think why she might have been out there? Was she meeting someone? History is an elective after sophomore year, so Fleur wasn't my student and this was the first time I met her."

"She wanted to take your class. When she found out a primordial was teaching history, Fleur tried to rearrange her schedule. She was even willing to drop one of her advanced charm classes because she could have taken them next year. She'd never be able to take a history class like yours again."

And I would have loved to have taught her. I loved teaching, especially when I had students who wanted to be there. All of my older students who had chosen to take history were thirsty for it. Most of them who were taking it as a prerequisite also were, but I had several who just didn't want to be in my class.

"Headmaster Krauss wouldn't let her. Fleur is insanely gifted with charms. She was already making a name for herself. Famous graduates reflect well on this university and it makes the headmaster look good. The previous headmaster was happy to just encourage Fleur and bring her new opportunities and let her choose if she wanted to take them. We don't like Headmaster Krauss. She kept putting all this pressure on Fleur and trying to micromanage her like she could get famous through her."

Lindsay Krauss had no business anywhere near the position she was currently in, but she wasn't the reason Fleur was on the dodgeball field. She couldn't currently leave her house. It wasn't just the sunlight. She had to be in constant contact with a certain potion being diffused into the air to get rid of that hex. The pustules would have made it insanely painful for her to move.

"Headmaster Krauss is a mediocre witch who wants to be as famous as my dear friend Minerva without working for it. She wasn't the reason Fleur was on the dodgeball field. I'm sure you saw the video. Everyone did. I'm filling in. Lindsay Krauss didn't do this, and she wasn't why Fleur was out there this late. She was probably going to be awful and controlling, but she had a vested interest in Fleur making it to graduation because it made her look good. Can you think of anyone who would do this to her?"

They all shared a look. They were grieving and in shock. In a perfect world, I'd be using my vast knowledge about death and what came after to help them deal with this. Any questions about who did it would have come after they were done grieving. But grief didn't work like that. You were never done with that. Every time I smelled lavender, it reminded me of my mortal lover who was slaughtered while I was away from her village, it punched me in the gut, and that happened thousands of years ago. I had to do this, so I didn't have this conversation with other students or have to bring the essence of more people who hadn't experienced life yet to the Aether.

"Everyone loved her. People tried to join our coven all the time, but Fleur always let them down in a way that they weren't mad about it after. It's just..."

"We have to tell them. This is the God of Death. Who do you want getting their hands on who did this? The Paranormal Investigation Bureau or a primordial? Because I don't want a trial and knowing they are in jail. I want cosmic justice."

This was probably delicate. I had this conversation before when I was more involved in this realm. My realm also wasn't utopia, even though I tried to make it as close as possible. Some people just wanted more, and I had criminals, too. I talked to the family and tried to find out who did it a lot.

"No judgment," I said. "I promise you that I've had this conversation since this universe was created and nothing you say is going to shock me. Also, know that nothing you tell me is going to make me think she had this coming or change my opinions about what a promising witch she was."

"Fleur was a terrible liar. She never lied about anything major, but sometimes she would try to say she wasn't hungry or tired or that something wasn't bothering her. Sometimes, Fleur would get burnt out and all she needed was a weekend off from charms to decompress. When we first joined her coven, we noticed right away. We started by asking and she'd always lie and say she was fine. We learned her tells when she lies about the small stuff. She played with her hair and scratched her nose. She never lied about the big stuff."

"Something was going on with her for the last two months. She wasn't taking as many charm orders, which wasn't a huge deal. We fully supported her charm business and how she wanted to run it. At first, it was a good sign because she worked herself too hard. But then she started lying, and she wasn't doing any of her usual tells. And we suspected it was something big.

"She'd say she was going to be in the library studying, but if we tried to meet her to carry her books, she wasn't there. Fleur would say she was meeting her charms mentor after dinner for extra work, but they usually met during her office hours.

"The charms professor adored Fleur, but she has five kids under the age of twelve. We thought it was weird she wanted to meet at night and frankly, Fleur never slowed down unless we made her and couldn't tell people no. We pulled her professor aside and asked her to take the meetings during school hours. She didn't know anything about night meetings with Fleur."

"Fleur wouldn't have cheated on us. We settled on our

coven, but we knew she was always getting requests because of how good she was with charms. Most of those people just wanted her because she was going to be famous. We always told her if she met someone who wanted her for her and she clicked with them, to bring them in and see how they vibed with the rest of us."

"We sat her down for a family talk and asked what was going on. We never called her out for lying if it was about minor stuff because she thought we were mad at her and she'd cry. She was lying about some pretty major stuff this time, but we still tried to be gentle about it, so we didn't upset her. She doubled down about it and I got angry. It wasn't like her and it wasn't like me, either.

"In any other situation, Fleur would have shrunk and started crying when she knew she was wrong and she thought we were mad. I actually was angry this time. Fleur fought back and kept insisting she really was in the library or with her professor. She was mad at us for doubting her.

"That was two nights ago, and she asked for space. We don't know why she was on the dodgeball field, but it probably has something to do with the nights she was supposed to be at the library or meeting her professor. We shouldn't have given her space. It was so out of character for her. We should have held her close and demanded she tell us the truth. We could have stopped this. We could have—"

The man broke down crying. This was the hardest part of death. The living always wondered what they could have done differently to keep their loved ones alive. Sometimes, there was nothing. It was their time, even if they were young and it was sudden.

Fleur was unnatural. I could taste it at the scene. She was supposed to grow old with her coven and take the supernatural world by storm with her charms. There was still nothing her coven could have done. Even if they surrounded her with love when she asked for space and didn't let her leave her dorm on Samhain, it probably would have just happened another night.

"Fleur didn't know why she was on the dodgeball field. She wouldn't have remembered how she had died, but she would have remembered why she was out there and who she was meeting. She would have been able to tell me about a new person in her life that might be a suspect. I don't think she lied to you about where she was those nights. I think she really thought that was where she was because her memory had been altered. She got angry with you because she really thought she was at the library or meeting with her professor."

"No. Professor Morningstar is one of my favorite professors. He went over those. Memory potions are considered dark arts. They weren't created with good intentions. They were only recently used for good to help people with extreme trauma, but you can't keep dosing people with them because there are side effects.

"Professor Morningstar went over those, so we knew what to look for. People who have been frequently dosed with forgetting potions start forgetting things they weren't coached to forget and they get a rash on their arms. Fleur wasn't doing that, and we saw her naked all the time. She was blemish free."

I was afraid of that. I wasn't teaching Dark Arts, but I studied them. Gabriel had some things in his family grimoire even I didn't know, but I knew the side effects if someone was abusing memory potions on someone. Forgetting little things happened first, and the rash came second. If Fleur had been given one enough that her coven had figured out she wasn't where she was supposed to be on two separate occasions, her arms would have been covered.

But memory potions weren't the only way to manipulate someone. It was a skill every god had if they cared to learn it. It was just like shapeshifting. We could do it if we wanted to. Most of us didn't try to learn that one because mortals tended to die. We could pull memories out of their heads, but it generally melted their brains. If there was a way to do that without horrifically killing them, no one I was friends with had practiced enough to figure that out.

Everyone I knew considered it a violation. Some of them had seriously sketchy consent issues when it came to people's bodies, but messing with someone's mind like that was too much for them.

And all I could do was promise her coven I'd find who did this and punish them. A killer on campus was going to cause a panic.

They couldn't know it was another god.

GEORGE

I hadn't swung by my aunt's cottage to see Freya and catch up, but history classes were supposed to resume with her teaching. So, color me totally shocked when I walked into history and my fucking dad was up there cosplaying as a professor. He was dressed like a hipster with his hair in a bun and Azren wasn't the only god at this academy who wore fake glasses.

I loved my dad, but who unleashed him on college students? He had endless patience with *his* kids, but not so much with other people's kids. Like, my mom wouldn't let him anywhere near our school if another kid was involved because several people would end up as roaches and he was the only one who could change them back. And my mom was the only person who could get him to unroach someone if he was mad at them.

Was the God of Death prepared to come in this class-room and change students back because my dad got irritated? Matilda, Mags, and I all stopped at his desk. He was pretending to read a thick history book, but I could see he had one of my mom's smut books for their book club hidden where the other students couldn't see it.

"You aren't Freya," I said.

"Definitely not. The board is abusing their headmaster being indisposed. Azren tried to tell the board they were really good at teaching, but hated administrative stuff and recommended Gabriel. They all but forced Azren to take over. Azren knew Freya needed this, so they brought her to this realm, and then the board basically told them they wanted a revolving door of gods so the students had a well-rounded history education.

"They wanted Azren to call in everyone they knew to do a week because it looks good for the Academy, but there's not that many of us here. So, I'm doing a bit, Loki will take a turn, Freya will be teaching, and Azren even got Odin to agree. It's so stupid. They wanted 'well rounded,' and they ended up with me and three gods from the Norse family."

"Please don't turn any of my classmates into rats."

"What does Azren do when they are disrespectful?"

"Throw shade," Matilda said.

"That's ridiculous," Dad scoffed. "You can shut that shit down immediately by transfiguring them into something really nasty. That Krauss girl should have spent time as a roach ages ago."

"Dad!" I pleaded.

"There are boys over there staring at you. Bring them over and introduce them."

West, Church, and Ren were all standing in the door staring at us. I mostly looked like my mom, but my eye color and eye shape were all my dad. Everyone knew my dad was a god thanks to Azren. My guys were expecting

Freya just like I was, but it wasn't too much of a leap that the gigantic god at the front of the room was my dad.

I'd successfully avoided my dad meeting any of my boyfriends, but they all ended up being assholes who were just using me for a favor from him. These guys? They were the real deal. These guys were 'meet the dad' kind of guys, so I called them over.

"Dad, this is Church, West, and Ren. They are important to me. Guys this is my dad."

My dad saw me signing. He didn't know who it was for, but he learned sign language with us when my mom was teaching it to us. My dad prided himself in all the languages he spoke and when my mom dragged him back into his body from the Aether, he dove into learning all the languages that developed after he left this realm.

He didn't know who he was signing to, but he started signing.

"Anyone who is important to George is important to us. You'll have to come by the library for dinner one night. I'll cook up something really special. Also, if you hurt her, her Uncle Loki and I will fuck your life up until we get bored with you, and then no one will find your bodies."

West just stood there grinning like my dad wasn't totally serious about that.

"No offense, sir, but Matilda already gave us that talk and she's terrifying under all that pink," West said.

My dad just leaned in and winked.

"Oh, we'd totally bring Matilda on as a paid consultant on this."

"No worries. She's my lioness. I have every intention of worshipping her," West said, giving my dad a knowing look.

Dad shot me a look, and I subtly shook my head to let

him know that only West was in on my secret. Dad would never press me about revealing it, but I always felt like I was letting him down because the whole reason I was a god was because of him. I was proud of my dad and what I was.

"Anyway, all of you need to come to dinner and meet the rest of the family so they can also threaten you. Azren told me that this job required punctuality and threatened to spank my essence without allowing me to use a safe word. You should all get to your desks so I can impress some college students. I haven't had my ass kissed by the masses in person for ages. Sit and make me feel special."

My dad got ridiculous when he wanted his ass kissed, but at least Balthazar wasn't here to egg him on. My mom usually reined them in and she wasn't here. Dad sat on the desk with his arms crossed staring the class down.

"What is the purpose of Chaos?" he asked.

Dexter's hand shot up.

"To fuck shit up?" he asked.

"Close. To fuck shit up with purpose. I'm a primordial. The universe couldn't have been created without a spark of Chaos. The universe continues to exist because of it. Azren said they were covering ancient civilizations. What happened to those civilizations that they are no longer around?"

Dexter's hand shot up again.

"Someone other than the pixie. We saw that video at the library. He has a handle on responsible chaos. That was perfection, by the way."

Kaylee hadn't come back to class yet, but her minions were sitting the next row over. They gasped and looked like they had been slapped that their professor not only saw the video, but he thought it was hilarious. Dad just ignored them, which was much better than turning them into mice.

I was surprised when Drake raised his hand because he never did that when Azren was teaching. Everyone kept telling me it wasn't Drake who murdered that witch, but I had my doubts. Someone had mangled Fleur's neck. Vampire venom was either agonizingly painful or erotic. It wouldn't have disabled her while someone cut her heart out. Basilisk venom would, I wasn't even all that sure if his venom wouldn't fuck up her memories.

A lot of people I trusted said it wasn't Drake, but no one told me why they thought that. Drake never even spoke in class, but Azren seemed sure. There were a lot of people at this academy who hated me, but they all didn't like me because Kaylee and Headmaster Krauss couldn't stand me.

No one seemed to hate me just for thinking I was a witch except for Drake. He was rude when I accidentally ran into him and he was constantly flashing snake eyes at me. Unless I was missing something and he just hated my face, there was a lot of bad history between Basilisks and witches that I shouldn't be the only one who was looking at him as a suspect.

I was going to look into Drake later.

"They were taken over by other civilizations or wiped out by some kind of natural disaster."

"That's true, but you're missing a key detail. They were wiped out by me. Their societies had become diseased. They were doing terrible things and claiming it was sanctioned by their gods. Their gods either couldn't or had no interest in controlling them. Primordials don't go around smiting entire villages because they misbehaved. It's not done.

"I'd introduce Chaos, whether it be flood, famine, or trying to incite a rebellion. The people could overthrow their leaders or the chiefs or kings could learn to make nice with their neighbors to share resources. Basically, I sprinkled some shit that was survivable and told them may the odds be forever in your favor.

"They didn't evolve. They kept doing exactly what they were doing and people died, left the settlement for greener pastures, or they weren't strong enough to fight back when they got attacked by someone they pissed off.

"I'm supposed to be teaching you history and we'll get to that, but you're all college students, so here's a life lesson. You're all probably a bunch of little shits and you're going to be that way until your brains finish developing. Chaos for the sake of destruction brings the attention of primordials and we will fuck you up. Chaos that brings growth and rebirth is like a phoenix rising from the ashes and if you absolutely need to be stupid, do that instead of the crap that permanently damages people. None of you are gods."

Drake's hand shot up again and my dad nodded to him.

"People are awful all the time and there's no godly retribution. There are ghosts everywhere that can't move on because humans slaughtered so many supernaturals on these grounds. No one exactly did anything when witches were slaughtering people like me for spell ingredients."

"That you can see. It's not just the ley lines or ghosts that make supernaturals gravitate to certain cities. Humans can't even see spirits. They were happy to plant crops over the mass grave they dug here. I made sure nothing grew here until they left and supernaturals reclaimed the land. Similar things happened in other supernatural cities. I was hanging out in the Aether at the time, but I still had a job.

"As for the witches and Basilisks, that was unfortunate. The Dark Arts didn't use to be so frowned upon and nearly everyone was dabbling in it. They weren't exactly checking people who went too far and were murdering people.

"Witches have gone by many different names in different cultures. Even when some humans were worshipping a god that told them witches were evil, they still lived side by side and were often healers for their village. The Dark Arts became taboo and frowned upon when humans caught dark witches doing something they really shouldn't and the witch burnings started.

"What the witches did to Basilisks was terrible, but it wasn't all witches. It was a select few with no respect for life and they ended up getting a lot of witches and a lot of innocent humans killed. Those witches also ended up getting a lot of knowledge lost.

"Not all the Dark Arts are evil. My wife is also handfasted to Professor Morningstar. His family grimoire has a lot of lost magic that can actually help people and no one has to die to make it. He's here teaching it instead of exploring the malicious shit on those pages. What those witches did was sheer evil, but it wasn't all witches. All witches ended up getting punished for it."

I didn't care if he caught me again and wanted to give me snake eyes. I knew about some of the dark shit in Gabriel's grimoire. He never let me read it, but he taught me some of the stuff that didn't kill anyone. My dad never really went over witches and Basilisks with me because there weren't any in my high school. They were pretty rare.

I didn't know everything he just told the class. I'm sure he blew a lot of witches' minds. I wasn't watching them. I was watching Drake. Did Drake have a vendetta against witches? He just sat back in his chair and caught me staring.

He flashed me snake eyes again.

OSCAR

George's dad was all over the internet and I looked him up again when we started talking. Nothing prepared me for how massive he was. Like, Azren was tall, but willowy. Reyson was seven feet tall and could crush my skull with his bare hands even if he wasn't a god.

And he seemed pretty cool. He invited us to the library for dinner. Yeah, he threatened divine justice against us if we hurt George. I couldn't tell if he was joking about that or not. He basically just told us to go fuck shit up responsibly.

Belladonna raised her hand. She'd been a complete asshole to George, but she seemed to have a lot of respect for the gods. Some of that could be ass kissing, but she didn't seem to want to kiss Headmaster Krass's ass.

"Excuse me, professor, but the Banshees shrieked last night and we aren't being told anything. They are telling us that it's nothing, but they don't scream unless someone died. Do you know what happened?"

He shot a look at his kids. From what they told me, they called home every night, and they didn't last night with everything going on. Reyson didn't know.

"I don't, but there's a faculty meeting at lunch. I'm sure I'll find out then. Ask your other professors. They might know. But you're right. If a Banshee screams, it's not nothing. You're dismissed. I need my kids up here before they leave."

We all followed George, Matilda, and Mags up to the front of the class. Reyson waited until everyone left. It meant a lot that he didn't kick us out, too. George said we were important, so he immediately decided we were family. And he was signing for me.

"Speak."

George and Matilda filled him in. We didn't know enough yet. I was guessing Azren did, but they were busy. We'd find out more later.

"Mm. I shouldn't have found this out from a vampire. Your mom is going to flip. No one told Gabriel, either. They've been trying to get him on campus for Samhain for years, but we have our own celebrations and ghosts to deal with at the library. I'm guessing Azren was dealing with that all night and that was why they didn't call me."

"The girl was well liked," Church said. "We can't think of who would want to do this to her."

"Someone with a problem with witches," George growled.

Probably so. I hoped she wasn't still thinking it was Drake. He didn't like them, but I thought that was more fear based. Drake didn't want anything to do with them. I had a feeling if Fleur had approached Drake, he would have just told her to fuck off and given her a little snake eye and tongue to scare her.

We hadn't just bonded in my dorm trying to talk to ghosts. We'd been talking in magical combat. Drake was cool. I liked him. I knew it wasn't Drake.

"Get to class," Reyson said. "Azren says that's important here. Watch your backs and don't be late."

We all took off in different directions because we had different classes. Drake caught up with me.

"You seemed to know something when Belladonna asked about the Banshees."

"Yeah, a witch got butchered on the dodgeball field last night. Azren came to get George, and we were with her. They brought us with them. I don't think Azren was expecting it to be that graphic out there."

Drake got angry and his eyes flashed to slits for a minute. He wasn't angry at me, so I just waited for him to explain.

"I don't get why Azren is all up her ass. I get that her dad is a primordial and they are friends, but she's just a witch. Azren had *no* business picking her to go investigate a murder. I get that you're into her and everything, but she's letting the weakest witch in this entire academy make her look bad and the only reason the headmaster got hexed instead of her was because a pixie stepped in. Azren is not going to get fired catching feelings for her, either."

"I'm missing something. You seem to think it should have been you that Azren came to get. I'm guessing there's a reason for that I don't know."

Drake wasn't unreasonable. Even his thing about his toenails wasn't that weird. There probably was some fucking weirdo skulking around campus wondering what they could do with those. He had reasons for asking me instead of a professor and after what happened with his parents, I didn't blame him.

"We're friends, right? Like, we aren't at the point where we're going to braid each other's hair, but I feel like we might get there one day. I just get those vibes. Can I trust you with a personal secret? Like, no telling anyone else?"

"Yeah, I feel that, too. For what it's worth, none of us have told anyone about your mom. Not even George."

"I was raised by a reaper on Azren's realm. Azren took an interest in me and was really involved when I was growing up. Azren isn't just here because of their feeling and what happened with that witch. They were supposed to be helping me figure out what happened with my mom. It was supposed to be us doing this together, but Azren replaced me with George. I know they have something cosmic going on with my mom, but I've known Azren since I was a baby. It's weird and hurtful they didn't trust me with this."

Yeah, okay. I got why Drake didn't like witches. I even got why he had a problem with George, even though I was pretty sure she didn't know any of that and probably would have called Azren out on it.

"I like Azren. They are a great teacher and I got to see them do the god thing in action. They seem like they give a shit, even though they've probably been at countless murder scenes. But excluding you from all this is a dick move."

"I know, right? Azren is brilliant, but they are forgetful and horribly disorganized. If they had just forgotten to come get me and gone out there alone, I wouldn't be mad about it. They went straight to George and brought all of you. West isn't even Azren's type."

I started laughing.

"West is pretty and an ally, but he's super hetero and very into George. Ren and I didn't want anything to do with her at first because West and Church were obsessed and it was highly annoying. They were writing a song for her after the first moon orgy. Ren said it was terrible, and it was probably the one time I was grateful I lost my hearing. Ren said he only knows five chords and he can't play those very well. We all love West, so we don't say anything when he plays the guitar or gets obsessed with a girl. I think George is it for him, though."

"She's just a witch," Drake grumped.

She was a hell of a witch. I was pretty sure she might even be the exception to Drake's witch thing if I could just get them in the same room and convince Drake to talk to her and convince George he wasn't a serial killer.

Azren put a whole kink in that by picking George over Drake when someone ended up getting murdered. George's dad said the gods weren't going around smiting people for shits and giggles. George was my girlfriend, but Drake was my friend.

Yeah, I was going to have a chat with Azren about it because Drake was clearly miserable.

AZREN

These fucking people. I hadn't been to bed yet, which wasn't the end of the world. I usually lived off four hours of sleep. It was the board and the Paranormal Investigation Bureau. They were losing their shit at how I handled this and I didn't do a damned thing wrong. I had an awful vampire with the board and an incubus with the Paranormal Investigation Bureau mansplain death to me and I wasn't happy about it.

They were angry I told Fleur's coven she was murdered, but what else was I supposed to do? They wanted me to let them think she just up and left and let every student on this campus think that no one died.

How was that supposed to work, anyway? Banshees were a type of Fae. Áine was a prolific goddess. She made the Seelie, Unseelie, Pixies, and Banshees under the Fae umbrella. Banshees didn't just keen when someone was going to die. They could sing to someone and help them through a difficult passing. A lot of them were healers.

But if they screamed? Someone was going to die.

I got that most college students could be idiots, but how did they expect to pull this off? The only person who wasn't talking down to me was former Headmaster Church.

"I'm sorry. I'm just one man and I can't control them."

"Freya is an amazing teacher. Reyson and Loki are good friends, but you don't really want them around college students. I didn't need to deal with that shit at six in the morning when I should have been handling a murdered student. Do you know how hard it is to get the God of Chaos out of bed? His wife holds a grudge."

"Ripley Bell? She was a hell of a student back in the day. So was her twin sister. How are her kids doing?"

"George is strong and smart and Matilda is going to run this entire planet one day. George is dating your grandson, by the way."

"Seriously?"

"We don't need to be talking about that. I'm pretty sure this has happened before. A student murder. I'm pretty sure it went down exactly like this and the university covered it up. Do you know anything?"

"It never happened under my watch, but there's a protocol for it. I never asked *why* we had it. It's different from any other student death," he said.

"Tell me."

"Well, revenants used to be a problem a long time ago. Not so much now. It's a lot harder to steal a body than it was in the past. Too many cameras and more security at the cemeteries. We get donated bodies for necromancy, but we don't get them that often. They get taught a lot of theory before they move on to practical work and they don't actually get a body until the last month of class. Each student gets one day and the Paranormal Investigation Bureau is there just in case.

"It does happen, just not as much as people think. If someone dies because of a revenant, the whole student body knows about it and we release a statement. Same if there's an accident in potions. If someone gets murdered on campus, we are supposed to pretend like they left and we don't know where they are, both to the students and their family. It's terrible, but it never happened the entire time I was headmaster. I honestly thought the policy was so bad because it never did and never would happen here."

"Mm. It did happen. I felt it but by the time I got here, it had stopped. Time moves differently in my realm. It's going to happen again. I have a feeling it's just getting started. Can you think of anything that happened nineteen years ago with a Basilisk named Artemis? Her son Drake is a student here now."

"Nineteen years ago, we had two attacks on campus. One involved an ancient cult and a few students died. I guess it did happen under my watch, but I knew who did it and they paid for it. You were here for that one because it was the first time I met you. Later that year, a student got shot in the fucking neck with a golden arrow. Several students saw and were able to save her. They never caught who did it. We haven't even taught archery on campus in ages.

"I remember Artemis. She was a promising student. I never found out why she left. She left for winter break and just didn't come back. Artemis dropped out online without ever speaking to anyone. I asked her roommate, and she said Artemis was acting strange before winter break, but she didn't know what was going on with her. Students do that sometimes. They get burnt out and drop out."

"Mm. She was murdered the next year. I'm trying to find out what happened for Drake."

"You aren't going to find that out in her school records. She was an exemplary student, but not even her roommate knew why she dropped out. The records were switched to electronic a few decades ago, but if you had that feeling before that, you'll need to go to the basement under Grimsbane Auditorium.

"When I was headmaster, I tried to get a project going where some of the scholarship students could do work-study and get paid taking all those records and digitizing them, but the board wouldn't approve it because they wouldn't be using magic to do it. Most of the board has never been poor or left their rich families and had to build themselves from nothing, so they don't realize money is money and some people are willing to take nonmagical jobs in a pinch to pay bills."

"Have I told you that you're the only board member keeping me sane lately?"

"An hour ago," he smirked.

"It's still true. And your grandson is going to be an amazing vampire one day."

"If not, George Bell will kick his ass. I know her mom and aunt."

I laughed because George would kick *my* ass, too. Literally. She already tried to assault me once. And since she wasn't a witch, it fucking hurt when she punched me in the face. There were only a few gods in existence that would dare punch Death in the face and she was one of them.

I was completely crazy about her.

There was a knock on my office door, so Church got up to leave. Oscar stuck his head in and I signed for him to come in. This was the first time I ever had him alone, and I had an idea. Gods could heal nearly any injury *if* it was able to be healed.

Vision and hearing were tricky. We could conjure things from nothing and we were capable of great magic. Reyson could only give familiars their bodies back because their essence was out of the Aether and he transfigured their animal into their old bodies. At least, I think. I still hadn't figured that out yet.

We couldn't regrow body parts. When we created life, it was either the traditional way of reproduction or building a creature from mud and feeding it our blood and breath. Giving someone sight or hearing back was possible if the raw materials were there to heal. Gods learned that the hard way when they were trying to perform miracles and ended up looking bad.

It might not work, but I could give Oscar his options. Before I could even say anything, he told me what he wanted.

"You need to apologize to Drake."

Drake and Oscar were friends? I approved. Drake had a lot of those back on my realm, but he hardly knew anyone here. He was so focused on school and his mom and paranoid about the witches that he was isolating himself.

"What did I do to Drake?"

"Seriously?"

"I honestly don't know. Drake is fiercely independent, and he hates it when anyone hovers."

"My roommates and I are the only people who know about his mom. He asked me to help him contact the campus ghosts. Church pissed off Bethany because she wouldn't help Drake and that's why she keeps punching him in the dick. Drake told me you helped raise him. He thought it was going to be you and him finding out what happened to his mom and stopping whatever was going to happen with your feeling. The first time the Banshees shrieked, you went straight to George instead of him. He's understandably hurt about that."

And the fact that he even told Oscar that meant he was definitely hurt. Drake stewed on his feelings until he sorted them. He never talked about them because Drake didn't trust anyone's opinions on his feelings except himself.

Drake was important to me. I didn't like knowing that I'd hurt him. But George was important to me, too, and I couldn't tell Drake or Oscar why she was who I went to last night because it wasn't my secret. George was dating Oscar, and she got spooked telling him. I'd never press George to tell her secret before she was ready, but Drake would understand if he knew and he'd be a lot more willing to talk to her if he knew she wasn't a witch.

George would realize Drake wasn't capable of that gruesome scene on the dodgeball field and all the people I cared about could be in the same room.

"There's a reason I went to George instead of Drake, but—"

"Don't tell me. It's not my business. You need to have this conversation with Drake. And you need to talk to George because I think she still thinks it was Drake who murdered Fleur. Drake is my friend, and he doesn't talk to a lot of people here. I get the feeling we could be good friends one day. I'm not going to betray that."

But I was supposed to? George didn't want anyone to know she was a god and Drake didn't want anyone to know he was raised by one or about what happened to his mom.

"I wanted to talk to you about your hearing," I signed.

Oscar looked uncomfortable, and I didn't want that.

"What about it?"

I tried to explain that I could *try* to heal him. It may or may not work. I couldn't tell if it was shitty to offer this and then it not work or never present him with an option that could change his life just because it might not.

"It might not work. I won't know until I lay my hands on you. The choice is yours."

Oscar chewed on his lip.

"Do it."

I walked around my desk and laid my hands on his ears. I let my healing light flow out and sought out the injury. It wasn't going to work. Oscar's eardrums had been obliterated. I couldn't put them back together.

"I'm sorry. There's not enough there. I can try conjuring cochlear implants."

"They said I wouldn't be able to try those for several months, but if you can do it without charging my abuela's insurance, then definitely."

"I'm sorry it didn't work."

Oscar just shrugged.

"It was worth a shot. Go talk to Drake."

I liked Oscar. He was good for Drake. And I definitely needed to make things right with Drake. I needed to tell him what I found out about his mom. I just needed to get myself out of all this stupid paperwork.

GEORGE

My mom raised her kids not to jump to conclusions when we didn't have all the evidence and to never accuse anyone without proof. I knew damned well I barely had anything on Drake. All I had was a weird neck wound and the fact that Drake didn't like me and had a reason to hate witches.

And deep down, I knew the neck wound *could* have been a vampire or a shifter. The whole scene was insanely violent. That didn't explain why she didn't fight when someone was cutting her heart out. *Something* paralyzed her. It could have been basilisk venom.

Not even my twin had my back. Apparently, there was some banter in magical combat that I missed when I was underneath a naked lion. Matilda said Drake might not like *me*, but he seemed cool. Mags was being an asshole and told me after Kaylee, I should be used to people not liking me. Then Mags told me this long, drawn-out story about some fancy lord back in her day who was probably perfectly lovely, but his face got on her nerves, so she couldn't stand him. Mags said I might just have one of those faces to Drake and that was why I kept getting snake eyes.

There were plenty of things Matilda and I would never agree on, but it was minor things about certain foods and music. She thought I looked hot in the style of clothes I liked wearing, but Matilda wouldn't be caught dead in them, I liked dresses sometimes, but not the type of dresses Matilda wore, even though she looked amazing.

But we had each other's backs on the major shit and I needed her to just support me and entertain the notion that it might be Drake. I could excuse my guys. I hadn't shared a womb with them.

So, I was going to do some digging on my own since I was, apparently, alone in this. I wasn't crazy. I wasn't going to march up to Drake in the dining hall and accuse him of horrifically murdering a witch everyone seemed to love. If it wasn't him, the entire campus was going to turn on him and her coven would probably kill him. I wasn't that kind of person.

I *was* the kind of person that found out which dorm he was staying in and when Drake and his roommate were going to be gone so I could go snooping for clues. I could portal in and out without being seen or picking a lock.

So, that's what I was doing. And I was surprised by this dorm. One side of the dorm had flannel sheets and posters from a vampire band Balthazar loved. The other side was insanely neat with silk sheets and these gorgeous framed paintings on the wall. There was a music stand by the desk and a violin case.

The side with the band posters had school books on their desk and nothing in the drawers except school supplies. There was a laptop, but it was password protected. My hacker vampire dad made sure we knew how to get around that kind of thing just in case we ever needed it, but I didn't exactly have time.

I was much more drawn to the other half of the room. There were books on that desk I'd never heard of and that said a lot considering my entire family were voracious readers and my mom was a librarian. There were books everywhere, even in the drawers. There was also a laptop that was password protected.

There was nothing under either mattress, so I moved to the closets. One was horribly disorganized, and it looked like whoever was using that one didn't like hanging up their clothes. There was nothing under the clothes, so I moved to the next closet.

I froze when someone came home while I was still in their closet. Like, completely froze. I should have portalled out immediately. I stayed hidden just in case I could see someone reveal their hiding place. The closet door was only open an inch, so I peered out. No one could see me and if they came toward the closet, I'd be gone before they ever found me.

It was Drake. The side of the room I was drawn to was apparently his. That didn't mean he wasn't a serial killer. Drake picked up the violin and started playing. I was utterly stunned. He was *amazing*. Between all my dads, my aunt's coven, and my extended family in Hell, I'd been exposed to everything from tribal music most people didn't know anymore, classical music, and vampire rave music.

I was pretty sure Drake composed this because I didn't know it. It was haunting and stirred up all kinds of emotions. Drake wasn't even a siren, and I wanted to go out there and be closer to him and his violin.

I almost did because he was *that* good. There was a

loose floorboard in his closet and my phone vibrated in my pocket when I stepped on it. Drake stopped playing.

"Who's there?" he demanded.

Shit!

I got myself out of his closet and back to my own dorm room. I looked down at my phone to see who was calling me. It was my cousin Freydis. She was a few years younger than me and a seer. Freydis desperately wanted to go to horseback riding camp. Her dad was created during the Viking era and Bjorn said, of course, his kid wanted to learn to ride a horse. My Aunt Ravyn fully supported her kid's hobbies.

Freydis got thrown from her horse and nearly died. If one of her dads hadn't been a god who could portal to her and heal her, she might have. But her magic awakened early. She was tutored by her dad and by the seers in hell. Freydis never told anyone exactly what she saw. It was always super cryptic because that's how everyone in Hell did it.

She was sometimes helpful, but a lot of her visions tended to revolve around my love life. She indirectly warned me that the guy I lost my virginity to was using me.

I'd call her back later. I was happy right now. I didn't think any of my guys were using me. No, I *knew*. But when a seer called you, you didn't ignore it.

DRAKE

Someone was in my closet. There was already one dead body on campus and I didn't intend to become the second. My fangs descended and I let them fill with venom. I wasn't fucking around with these witches. I'd happily go to jail if they didn't believe me it was self-defense.

But when I flung my closet door open, there was no one in there. My closet wasn't like my roommate's. I hung my clothes up and there wasn't anywhere to hide in here. I only knew one person who could be there one minute and gone the next. Azren just *would not* be caught dead hiding in a closet.

Gods were different when it came to sexuality and gender. Azren had never been in *any* closet. They wouldn't be spying on me in mine. If Azren wanted to talk to me, they would have just appeared on my bed and made themselves at home.

I didn't imagine it. I got wrapped up in my violin and I'd

worked on that piece for ages. I just needed to put the final touches on it and it was done, but it hadn't come to me yet. It would have had to have been a *loud* noise to pull me straight out of my playing.

My roommate's closet might be a disaster, but he never left food out. We didn't have rats. That was when I noticed one of the floorboards was crooked. Bethany said this was my mom's old room, and the ghosts put me in here to help me. Was this Bethany? Because it certainly wasn't Azren. I was furious with them right now, but they would have stayed.

I fell to my knees and removed the floorboard. There was a dusty, ornate box at the bottom. There were snakes carved on the box lid. My heart was beating in my throat. This box belonged to a Basilisk. Other races used snakes, but these were the serpents I could shift into if I wanted.

I gingerly pulled the box out and reverently carried it to my bed. This could be my mom's. I didn't have anything of hers. I was taken to Azren's realm with a stuffed toy and that was it. I studied the box. It had a blood lock.

Headmaster Krauss became famous with a spell to pick a blood lock, but it involved so much blood, you could die. If this was my mom's box, then it should just take one drop of my blood to open it. If it wasn't her box, it would probably kill me. I couldn't risk it because I didn't *know*.

It was a start. I wanted to go tell Azren, but I was just so *mad* at them. Azren came to me, though. They appeared on my desk chair in a cloud of black smoke.

"Drake, I wanted to apologize for last night. I didn't forget about you. I would have brought you both, even though I know you don't like her, but I made a choice. It was violent, Drake. Someone cut out that witch's heart while she was still alive. You saw your parents getting murdered. You don't remember any of it because you were just a baby, but I could tell it was going to be bad before I went out there. I didn't want to trigger any memories by bringing you out there."

"Shouldn't it be up to me what I can handle? Maybe I'll remember who did it."

"It doesn't work like that, Drake. You aren't going to remember their face. You're more than likely just going to get panic attacks and nightmares."

I grunted. Azren was probably right. They knew more about this shit than I did. I still didn't see what was so special about George Bell.

"I did find out something about your mom. It's not a lot. The only person on the board that I don't want to do terrible things to their essence was the headmaster when she was here. There were two attacks that year. Two students were murdered in one, but I know who did that. I was involved in punishing the person responsible.

"A few months later, someone was shot in the neck with a golden arrow, but there were witnesses. No one died that time. A few months later, your mom went home for winter break and never came back. She dropped out online and her roommate didn't even know why. Headmaster Church said Artemis was a promising student who was doing well academically. He asked around when she dropped out, but no one knew why."

"Someone was in my closet. When I went to check it out, one of the floorboards was disturbed. I found this. It has Basilisks carved on it. The ghosts said they put me in her old room. This could be hers."

"Well, why haven't you opened it?"

"Blood lock."

"I'm immune to witch magic. We can use my blood without killing me."

It would be so easy to let Azren do this, but Azren was always telling me how stubborn I was.

"If it's my mom's blood lock, it should be me that opens it. I don't know if I'm ready just yet."

It didn't make sense, and I knew that. I should be giving this box to Azren and finding out what was inside. I didn't want the lock broken if I could help it. If it was my mom's, she locked this and hid it under the floorboards for a reason. It should stay locked once I got into it. I needed to work up the nerve to prick my finger on the lock.

"Don't do that without me. Text me when you're ready to open the box and I'll be here to heal you if it's not your mom's."

I wanted it to be my mom's. I *needed* it to be hers. Azren could heal me no problem if it wasn't, but I wasn't ready to find out that the box under the floorboards wasn't my mom's.

CHURCH

The ghosts on this campus were horrible, petty bitches. Every time I relaxed or let my guard down, Bethany popped out of the floor or wall and punched me right in the dick. West made an emergency trip into town and picked up cock protection from a store that sold dodgeball gear and it wasn't even fair!

Her hand passed right through the cup and still connected with my dick. And it wasn't like I could grovel and apologize, even though I was right for what I said, because she didn't stick around after the dick punching.

At this point, a ghost had touched my dick more than my girlfriend and I couldn't remedy that because my cock hurt all the time. Azren was healing me when they could, but it was like Bethany was watching for godly intervention on my dick and would nut punch me again when they left.

My phone rang before class and it was my grandfather.

"Hey, what's up?"

"Watch yourself on campus. There's a murderer on the

loose and the board isn't happy Azren didn't follow protocol and now the students know."

"That's a good thing, though. People can watch their backs now."

"Exactly. The board doesn't agree with me on this. Some of them are saying Azren isn't fit to be headmaster, which is what Azren told them the first time, but they are greedy. If they move Azren back to teaching history, then they can't say they had one god as a teacher in residence and three other gods who came in to guest lecture for a few weeks while that awful woman heals."

"No one likes Headmaster Krauss except her daughter and the people who are kissing her ass for letters of recommendation and favors."

"Oh, I was headmaster when she was a student. I told them to go with Gabriel Morningstar, but they don't want to pull him from Dark Arts and picked Lindsay over him because she's alumni. Speaking of, I hear Gabriel Morningstar might be your father-in-law soon."

I groaned.

"How'd you find out?"

"Well, I would have found out when you brought her home to meet me, but Azren ratted you out. You need to bring her home soon."

"I think I have a hive," I whispered.

This was the first time I said it out loud. We were technically George's coven, but we were also my hive, West's pride, and Oscar's coven, too. That was just how it worked. And they were all fantastic.

"Seriously? Bring them around for dinner one night. We'll have to plan something. Azren also says you are doing well in their class. I'm so proud of you."

That meant a lot because I certainly knew my parents

weren't. They'd disowned me as soon as I hopped on that plane to America. I had one *email* from them telling me that I was no longer their son and hadn't heard a damned thing from them since. Good riddance. I didn't miss them.

I wasn't embarrassed bringing my hive to meet my grandfather. I knew a lot of people were afraid of him, but he'd always been good to me.

"Hey, do you remember Bethany, the campus ghost?"

"Please tell me that you didn't piss her off."

"Uh, kinda?"

"Apologize. A lot. Grovel if you have to."

"She keeps flying off after she assaults me."

"Oh, you pissed her off, pissed her off. She likes trinkets. Leave some out for her."

I nodded. Ren could steal those for me. His fox was a little klepto that needed to steal for the people he cared about. I thought I was included in that. Unless Bethany thought that was a shortcut and I needed to steal for her myself?

Why was this my life right now?

I excused myself because I needed to get to class, but I always looked forward to talking to my grandfather.

WEST

Campus was pretty sour right now. Everyone knew about Fleur. They didn't know how it happened since I guess Azren didn't get graphic. The board censured Azren. They told her coven, but they couldn't tell the students over morning announcements. Azren was avoiding everyone.

My girl's dad was pretty damned cool. *Very* different from Azren and definitely the God of Chaos. Reyson asked us to call him by his first name like Azren did and seemed to take an entirely different view of the world. Azren seemed to view it as something to study and Reyson looked at it like a playground.

We were finally back at my happy place—magical combat. I was okay with not being a student here. All that homework seemed like a nightmare. But I could participate in magical combat because Zion liked me and knew damned well that my girl could kick any ass in this class.

Before Zion paired us up, he just crossed his arms and glared at us.

"You're all terrible, but some of you show promise. Azren might not want the headmaster job, but they are pretty fucking effective. Next Friday, I'll be holding try outs for the Academy dodgeball team. I'll—"

I shrieked. I couldn't even try out for the fucking team, but I could cheer Oscar and George on. And my girlfriend playing dodgeball? Total spank-bank material. That was hot as fuck. Zion just chuckled at me.

"Yes, I'll expect that kind of enthusiasm at try outs. We're going to do something different today. Physical fitness. Some of you are seriously out of shape for supernaturals. Since you *should* have already warmed up and stretched, I want you running laps until I get bored. Lion, go run with them. Your energy makes me nervous."

"Did he notice me again?" I whisper-yelled to George.

"Totally did, but you're hard not to notice," she said, pinching my bottom.

Her phone went off in the middle of class and Zion's gaze zeroed in on her.

"Is there something more important than magical combat?"

"No, sir. My cousin keeps trying to contact me. Sorry. I'm turning my phone off and I'll call her tonight. I'm ready to run."

"And try out for my dodgeball team?"

"Oh, shit yes!"

"Good. Now *move!*"

We all started running laps. Zion wasn't kidding. We ran until he got bored and a lot of people in our class were out of shape. Zion just stood there glaring as some people started lagging behind and walking. They probably wouldn't be trying out for dodgeball.

"I said run, not walk!"

"We're sirens, you toad! We're meant for swimming not running."

"Well, you might get caught on land away from water. What are you going to do?"

"Sing my way out of it!"

"Can you sing after you've fought your way to safety? *Make* me let you stop running. Everyone, you're running until the sirens can get me to let you quit."

I was starting to get how Zion Skinner's brain worked. Running was easy for me. I'd always done it. Oscar and I went running every day before breakfast. It wasn't just because I was a lion, either. There were plenty of lazy lions. I just liked it because I always had a lot of energy. Zion wanted us running for dodgeball tryouts, but he made it a lesson.

The first people who complained were going to have to use their magic to fight him and get him to let us stop. We'd spent months fighting each other in controlled situations, but he stepped up the game. Zion got their heart rates up and was going to make them fight him.

Genius.

The sirens stopped to catch their breath so they could sing and Zion barked at them to keep going. They shot him a death glare, but I got it. If they were in a real fight, they weren't going to be able to stop. They'd have to push through.

They finally did it. It was breathy and not as good as if they were singing at a moon orgy, but they sang their desire to stop running. Zion's mental shields were strong, but they eventually cracked and he let everyone stop.

"Congratulations. You just survived being chased by a bear and getting him to stop."

"But you weren't chasing us, sir."

"Pretend it was a fucking metaphor, you turnip. You were running until I let up. It's not rocket science. I weep for the future. You're dismissed. If you're looking to try out for dodgeball, I'll be running drills on the dodgeball field before dinner every night until tryouts to get you ready since some of you might be rusty since high school. I was also told to pass along the message from Professor Norwood that she'll be running drills at the same time and cheerleading auditions will happen Saturday."

This time, it was Matilda and several of the girls that started screaming. Cheerleaders were fucking badasses. They flung each other up in the air and did all kinds of stunts. I was glad Azren pulled some strings and got a squad. The dodgeball team could play without one, but there were several superb athletes in this school who weren't good at dodgeball that now got to show off their skills.

I slung my arm around George's shoulder and we started walking back to the dorms to shower.

"Why is your cousin calling when you are in class?"

"She's probably seen something."

I knew all about her cousins. I made it a point to learn the names of all of her family. So, it was *that* cousin. The one that saw the future.

"Yeah, you should definitely call her back."

"Every time she gets a vision, it's about my love life."

I nipped her ear.

"She's probably seen that I'm absolutely crazy about you. We all are."

And her cousin had better not tell her a fucking thing different.

DRAKE

I was sitting at dinner by myself again. It didn't bother me at first, but now that I was friends with Oscar, I wished I could sit with him and his friends. George hadn't joined them yet, but she would. So, I sat alone and was just content with the knowledge I found that box. I could feel it that it was my mom's. It had to be.

I had my head down scrolling through social media while I ate my food. I felt the air stir as someone sat across from me. I looked up and smiled because I thought it was Oscar. I immediately frowned when it was George Bell sitting across from me.

"What the fuck do you want?" I demanded.

"Look, you don't like me and I'm still not all that sure you didn't murder that witch on the dodgeball field. Everyone says you didn't and my cousin says I'm supposed to talk to you. She's a seer, so I do what she says."

I scoffed.

"There's no such thing as seers. How do I know *you* didn't kill that witch? Maybe you were jealous."

Was she serious right now? Her cousin? Really? That was the biggest load of bullshit I'd ever heard. Maybe she did murder that witch and now she was trying to frame me for it by spinning the Basilisk revenge angle. She was the one who came into *my* personal space and interrupted my dinner, but she had the nerve to look irritated with me.

"Okay, so I *hate* name dropping my family, and fuck you for making me, but my uncle is Loki. Loki made seers when Odin and everyone else was hunting him down for arranging Baldur's murder to get back at them for killing his kids. The seers told Loki that Odin was going to catch him no matter what he did and when it was coming, so Loki put the seers in another dimension. That's why *you* don't know they exist. Hell has demons that can train on that kind of thing, but aren't like my Uncle Bjorn.

"My Uncle Bjorn had sex with my Aunt Ravyn and made my cousin Freydis, who is also a seer. There was an unfortunate incident with a horse and now my cousin can see the future. She mostly sees my love life, but I'm pretty sure this vision was about you."

That was *a lot,* but I didn't see what that had to do with me. Azren was rarely in the dining hall except for lunch, but they seemed to be here tonight. They zeroed in on us right away and floated over to our table. I knew Azren was tutoring her, but she didn't know who I was to Azren. Azren might be a little more interested in her than I would have liked, but they wouldn't have told her my business.

I knew that look. Azren didn't know if this was a good thing or we were about to start brawling and he'd have to heal my venom from her system so she didn't die.

"What's going on here?" Azren purred.

"Some nonsense about cousins and Viking seers."

"Not nonsense. Her Uncle Bjorn is an amazing seer. The rest of the gods didn't even attempt to create them because they thought flooding them with visions of the future would drive them insane. Lilith made it a possibility with her demons with the right training and Loki figured out the recipe to make seers without driving them insane. If Bjorn or his daughter has a message for you, then you should listen," Azren said, sitting next to me.

"You can pass your message, but I'm not dating you if it's about your love life again."

George just rolled her eyes.

"Who says I want to date you, either? You're mean for absolutely no reason. I haven't done shit to you. Anyway, my cousin says I'm looking for answers and so is the snake. We're only going to find those answers by working as a team. Now that I've actually spoken to you, I'm not looking forward to it any more than you are. The *only* reason I sat there while you were being rude to me for no reason is because the only way I can figure out the answers to what I want is to help you find yours."

"Guess you can't kill me now!" I sneered.

"What the fuck are you talking about? I would have just got up, left, and avoided you after that. What kind of psycho kills someone for being rude? Even my dad just turns them into bugs for a little while unless they hurt someone. What in actual fuck is wrong with you?"

"I'll bet the first thing you ask if I agree to work with you is to meet in my dorm room so you can steal hair from my brush or scour around for my toenail."

"First of all, that's fucking gross. Secondly, my dad has been teaching students to safely use and fight Dark Magic. I grew up in the Library of the Profane. If I had done *anything* downstairs to learn magic my parents didn't teach me, my mom would have lost her job and we would have lost our home. What *exactly* about any of that makes you think I'm the kind of person who is interested in stealing hair and toenails?"

"Drake?" Azren said. "She's right. Not all witches are bad, just like not every Basilisk are serial killers. You know they once said that to justify killing your kind. I know your train of thought right now is that you have other options to find out what you need, but seers get their visions from the Fates for a reason. No god can compete with that. George is how you get your answers and I can vouch for her. I think the two answers are tied together."

Fuck my life. Azren was my mentor and had never steered me wrong before. They even helped me with girls back on their realm. They wouldn't tell me to work with a witch unless it was safe.

But why did it have to be the witch that was stealing Azren from me?

GEORGE

Drake was infuriating. I knew Freydis couldn't control her visions, but I think I preferred her cryptic messages that a guy I was into was actually a dickface to this one. Kaylee and Lindsay Krauss didn't like me because of my relationship with Minerva and they ended up losing out because theirs was lacking. There were other people who didn't like me but it was usually because I worked my ass off at school and dodgeball and they wanted me to be mediocre.

Drake didn't even have a good reason for hating me. He thought I was a witch, so I was automatically lumped in with witches from a long time ago who did terrible things to Basilisks. Azren talked him into working with us, but Drake couldn't be bothered to tell me what I was supposed to be helping him figure out before he stormed out of the dining hall.

"How am I supposed to work with him?" I ranted in my dorm room. "He hates modern witches because of something that was done in the past. I don't even know what I'm supposed to be helping him with!"

"Because he's not ready to tell you," Matilda said. "It was different for my dad because the demon who bought him when he was young treated him like a son. It was different for my grandparents. They were bought and raised to be slaves. They were forced to have babies with people they didn't know to make someone rich and their babies were immediately taken away from them.

"The Hellhounds are free now and have the same rights as demons, but that didn't erase their trauma. Some of them went to therapy so they could be in the same room with demons without killing them. Some didn't and never really got over it, so they avoid going to places a lot of demons would be. It's not just the demons that owned them and mistreated them. It's *all* demons.

"You don't know Drake or what his past is. *You* are not even a witch, but you've been bullied by a few. It's not outside the realm of possibility that he went through something terrible with witches. I talked to him in magical combat when he was sparring with Oscar. He was relaxed and having fun.

"You have two choices here. You can keep pretending to be a witch and show him that not all witches are after his parts or you can make an exception for him and take off your necklace in front of him and let him see the truth," Matilda said.

"You're going to have to pick fast, cupcake," Mags said. "We might not know what Drake is trying to figure out, but you're trying to figure out who murdered Fleur and stop it from happening again."

"I wish the demons hadn't trained Freydis to be so fucking cryptic," I sighed.

Because it would really help me if I knew what Drake was trying to figure out and how it was tied to the campus murders. Since that the Fates had spoken through my cousin, stopping the campus murders was now on my shoulders instead of Azren's and I couldn't do it without helping a rude Basilisk who hated me for something I didn't even do.

"That's a safety measure. I was visiting Hell with Dad when Freydis was there studying. The Hell seers are different from Freydis and Uncle Bjorn, but it's this massive responsibility. The Fates give the seers the visions so they can change them. If they give someone the entire vision, they'll focus on the wrong things. They all think changing one minor detail will make the outcome go in their favor. If you give it to them like a riddle, they focus on the big picture and the tiny details. They are more likely to get successful results changing the vision."

I threw up my hands.

"She just said I needed to work with the snake. That could have been the only Basilisk at the academy or a metaphor. Freydis has a massive imagination, and she keeps begging to join smutty book club. Remember when she called me when I was thinking about losing my virginity? All she said was *don't trust the weasel.* She likes animal metaphors. What if I made a whole-ass scene in the dining hall and she didn't even mean Drake?"

"Sit down. You're making me nervous," Mags said. "Sometimes, I wish I could conjure shit like you can because I'd make a Pez dispenser that shot a Xanax straight down your throat. You get extra high-strung sometimes because of that godly DNA."

"Oh, shut up. I do not."

"You do, too," Matilda said. "Literally, no one at this

school can hurt you physically. You're immune to Drake's venom. All he can do to you is be mean and my twin sister just does not let men be rude to her. Bell women don't get butthurt. We get even."

"You're thinking you have to sit there and take his vitriol because it's the only way to stop anyone else from getting murdered, but you don't. Drake isn't getting his answers without you, either," Mags said.

"Drake doesn't like you, so clearly he has shitty taste, but I've talked to him in magical combat. He's not a bad person or completely unreasonable. Drake might not like witches, but I didn't get vibes from him that he's going to let students get murdered because he's refusing to work with you. Just remind him of that. Or you could cosmically put him in his place by taking off your necklace and blowing his mind that he's been mouthing off to a fucking god."

That would be satisfying. I've never pulled the god card. I had never once considered whipping my necklace off to put Kaylee Krauss in her place. In a way, I got why she hated me. I wasn't even thinking when I pointed out her great aunt was allergic to strawberries when she was talking about eating strawberry cake at Minerva's house several nights a week.

I was a kid. I wasn't thinking that Kaylee was lying to look better because she was also a kid. All I was thinking about was how bad it would be if Minerva ate strawberries. A few people teased Kaylee about it. It would have eventually blown over, but then Minerva's will was read and I got everything Kaylee and Lindsay thought they were due.

Kaylee and Lindsay earned everything they got or didn't get when it came to Minerva, but I got why they thought that was all my fault. They were mostly annoying.

But Drake? I didn't do anything to Drake. Until I crashed his dinner, I'd never even spoken to him before. He hated me because he thought I was a witch.

Drake made me want to take off my necklace and put him in his fucking place.

GEORGE

My head was a lot clearer after I'd gotten some sleep. My brain had time to marinate on everything Matilda and Mags tried to tell me. Matilda was right. We shared a womb, but our ancestors had very different experiences. My dad didn't have parents. He was just created one day before the universe. I didn't have a set of grandparents from him.

Matilda's dad and grandparents used to be someone's property. Bram was raised like a son and didn't have to go through the things the other Hellhounds did. Her grandparents did though, and they didn't like to talk about it.

Drake didn't know me, but I also didn't know Drake. Now that I'd slept on it, Drake's reaction to witches was weird. Magic with Basilisk parts was forbidden before Europeans ever came to the New World. People still broke them, but then about one hundred and fifty years ago, they tightened the laws and made the punishments stricter.

Like, Drake was so paranoid I was going to steal his hair and toenails and honestly, I wouldn't put it past some people, but even spells where a Basilisk sold someone hair or nail clippings willingly was a life sentence because the potions that were made with them were usually deadly or had horrific results.

I could be butthurt that Drake was rude to me or I could try to nip it in the bud and find out why Drake was so paranoid about it. So, when I got to the dining hall, I interrupted Drake's breakfast, too.

"Yeah, no. You don't have to like me, but the Fates decided we're a team now, so you aren't eating alone anymore. We've got shit to figure out. You might think I'm terrible, but the other people I sit with are pretty fucking amazing. They are helping me and they'll help you, too."

Drake scowled at me, but he picked up his tray and followed me to my table. And apparently, all my boyfriends knew and liked Drake. Drake and Oscar had a secret handshake. When did that even happen?

"Baby Drake!" West boomed. "Welcome to the team. Church will choose his words much better if you need to talk to ghosts again."

"You got my boyfriend's dick repeatedly assaulted by a ghost?" I hissed. "I had plans for it."

"That wasn't Drake," Ren said. "Church's dick woes are all on him. Everyone who's graduated middle school knows not to insult a ghost."

"Wait, the ghosts are messing with your dick?" Drake asked.

"Bethany keeps popping out of the floor and punching me right in the cock. I keep hoping she'll get bored with my dick, but so far, no luck."

"In all fairness, your dick is pretty fabulous," I said.

Matilda gagged.

"Excuse me, but there are lesbians trying to enjoy their breakfast over here."

"Dick punching is funny. Sorry, Church," Mags said.

Church moaned and adjusted himself.

"Azren says they've been both male and female, so you should know they said getting your nuts smashed is the same as you getting punched in the tit. So, think about that when you laugh every time Bethany dick punches me."

"Only little bitches punch you in the tit or pull your hair," Matilda said.

"Gotten into a lot of brawls?" Drake asked, cocking an eyebrow at my twin.

"Hell, yeah. My twin sister is a badass who could magically kick anyone's ass but has big opinions about accidentally hurting people. I'm technically her big sister, so I've defended her honor and kicked some asses. George finds most shit annoying, but if she moves past annoyance, she'll throw some magic at you and embarrass the shit out of you. I'll make it hurt. I keep waiting to pair up with Kaylee in magical combat so her mom doesn't get all malignant about it."

I shot my sister a grateful look. Underneath all that posturing, big sister talk, and the threat to maim Kaylee when she could get away with it, that entire speech was meant for Drake. My sister wanted me to take the necklace off, but she'd never pressure me.

So, she tried to paint me as the kind of person who restrained themselves to avoid hurting people. Which was true, but I couldn't say that without sounding like I had a fat head. Drake at least seemed to relax a little.

"Tell me about this big mission I'm supposed to be helping you on."

"It's the murdered witch," I said.

"The one you thought I killed."

Drake didn't look angry. He seemed amused that I even went there.

"There was a weird wound on her neck and she didn't fight back when her heart was being cut out. I thought Basilisk venom."

Drake sat up straighter.

"Were there black spiderweb veins on her neck?"

"Actually, no."

"Then it wasn't a Basilisk. Our venom leaves behind telltale signs."

"Sorry then. You're actually the first Basilisk I've met, and we didn't go over venom in high school. My dad actually went over some things I didn't know in history. It was just a guess and I can admit when I'm wrong."

"Um. Thanks. Most poisons that would have paralyzed her would have left something behind. They would have turned the wound black around the edges or had some kind of spiderweb. If she had ingested it, it would have been trickier, but if it was introduced through her neck, you could tell."

"It didn't look like a vampire bite and it certainly didn't look like a needle, either," Church said.

"I can't think of a reason anyone would lay there while someone was cutting their heart out, but poison leaves behind signs," Drake said.

"I don't think it was a student," Ren said. "It looked surgical. No one here knows how to do that. Healers have to go to another school to learn how to do that."

"We need to talk to Azren," West said.

"We definitely do," Drake said.

Was Drake friends with Azren, too? Was Drake friends

with all my boyfriends? He was much less hostile over breakfast. It was a start. Matilda and Mags were right. I still didn't know what I was helping him with, but he was definitely willing to help us.

It was a start.

WEST

Sometimes, you just met someone and knew they were your people. Lions were super intuitive about that. When I met Oscar for the first time, I *knew* I had to sign for him. I clicked with Ren as soon as I met him. I knew George was my lioness almost immediately. I just needed to convince *her* of that and do a deep dive into academy rules to make sure I didn't have to be sneaky about it. I vibed with Church right away because he had insanely good taste in women.

And then there was Baby Drake. I knew we should adopt him as soon as Oscar brought him to our dorm room. He had that tortured soul with a dark past thing going on, but Drake was also very ginger, so I knew when he let go, he was going to be a lot of fun.

But there was the small problem of Drake and George. George didn't think he was a serial killer anymore. She just thought he was insanely rude, though he was getting slightly better about it. George was being hostile right back.

And I could fix all that so they could hate fuck and Drake officially became one of us, but I'd have to betray George and I'd never do that to her.

So, I'd been meddling and redirecting the conversation so they could get to know each other when we hit a snag trying to figure out who the murderer was. Because everyone knew about Drake's mom except the one person the Fates said was going to get him those answers. Drake didn't trust her yet, and I wasn't spilling Drake's secrets, either. *I* wasn't that person, but I was really good at making people comfortable enough to talk.

Like for instance, Drake just revealed he wasn't just a really ginger dark soul with a twisted past. He was a fucking musician and composer. That was hot as fuck and I was very much only into women. It also gave me an idea.

"Did you bring any of your instruments with you?"

"I play a lot of them, but the violin is my favorite. It's also the most portable and easiest to fit in a small dorm room. My roommate is a bit of a player and is rarely home, so I have a lot of time to play and work on my compositions."

A violin was *perfect.* And this was the official test if Baby Drake was really as decent as I thought he was. Because I was excusing the shit out of him being malignant to my lioness.

"Would you be opposed to Oscar laying his hands on your violin while you play? The vibrations may be a way for him to enjoy music again."

"Dude, of course. If it works, I'll play whenever he wants me to. Is anyone trying out for dodgeball? Because I am."

"George and I are," Oscar said. "What position do you play?"

"I'm not trying out for the cheerleading team, but I'm the official coven cheerleader," Ren said.

"My father liked watching dodgeball matches from private boxes, but he always used it to network and close deals. He rarely paid attention to the game. He thought people of our station watched games from expensive private boxes, but we were above playing the game ourselves. My grandfather encouraged me when I ran and taught me how to just enjoy the game, but I'm terrible at playing it. I'll be joining Ren cheering the rest of you on."

"I play goalie. They have to watch me if they want to get the ball past me, but if I can snare their gaze, they miss. If they try to avoid looking at me altogether, it's usually a wild throw that I can block."

I grabbed Drake and gave him a very straight, platonic kiss on the mouth because those kinds of goalie skills were sexy as fuck and should be rewarded by a kiss from a very sexy lion. Oscar was good enough to go pro. George was a secret god and probably had some mad dodgeball skills. Drake could fuck up someone's good intentions to score a goal by giving them Basilisk stink eye. And we had Zion Skinner coaching them.

If Drake and George ended up hate fucking, I'd have three of the most important dodgeball positions in my pride. That was sexy as hell. We'd also catch a murderer and get Drake some closure.

We just needed Drake to get over his shit with witches and then do some serious groveling to George. My fantasies about having a pride full of dodgeball players could wait.

Even if Drake and George never hate fucked, we needed them to get along because the Fates had just gotten involved.

GEORGE

Some people would feel weird if their dad was asked to guest lecture their history class just for being a god. Some people would be abusing that for clout. I was grateful he was here. He'd been asked to do this several times when I was growing up and he always said no. He was good at it and he looked like he was having a blast. Dad hadn't transfigured any of my classmates either.

And my dad had certain abilities as the God of Chaos that Azren didn't and I'd only have if I was close to my dad. I stopped by his desk before history.

"Dad, I need your help. I need you to look at some possibilities."

My dad couldn't necessarily see the future, but he was literally created to sow chaos to balance the universe. He had to be able to see the big picture. He could run scenarios in his head and see the possible outcomes. Dad wasn't trying to slaughter people for no reason. He needed to know exactly what kind of Chaos to bring.

My dad leaned in to whisper.

"You can do that, too, now. I'm borrowing Azren's office while they are doing the headmaster thing. Come see me after class."

"Thanks, Dad."

"Bring those boys to dinner soon."

I heard a scandalized gasp. Kaylee was back in class finally. She seemed surprised my dad was here. I guess the board wasn't keeping Headmaster Krauss abreast of what was going on here. Oh, this was going to be good.

I never knew what he said to her, but my dad pulled Lindsay Krauss aside after they sued me and whispered in her ear. Kaylee and Lindsay left me alone for a bit after that. Lindsay had her big reveal with the blood lock spell she stole from Minerva and Kaylee was transferred to a private school where all the snotty kids who thought they were special because their ancestors used to be lords went. They started up again when I got to college because I guess they thought my daddy wasn't going to find out.

My dad had avoided turning anyone into a bug so far, but everyone had been on their best behavior. Everyone seemed to love him, which wasn't shocking. My dad was the best. Kaylee's minions weren't showing him the same disrespect they showed Azren, and that probably had a lot to do with Kaylee not being here.

"You're late," Dad snapped at Kaylee.

Kaylee looked so confused. She glanced down at her phone.

"But I have two minutes until class starts."

"I helped invent time. I think I'd know if you're late," Dad sniffed.

I was trying so hard not to laugh because my dad knew damned well she wasn't late. He had a cell phone and he could tell time from the position of the sun and moon. So could I because he taught me. He was giving her a hard time because he saw that video. A random roaching might happen, too.

"But—"

"Not only are you disrespecting something I helped create, but you're wasting everyone's time arguing with me about it. Get out of my class and go do something useful. You have the kind of face that just pisses me off and you're *late.*"

The entire class was silent and Kaylee just stood there gaping like a fish. We all knew she wasn't late, even my dad. Dad could be Petty Betty sometimes. Yeah, he *could* have let her in class, waited for her to open her mouth, and then roached her. She would have run straight to mommy when he turned her back and the board may or may not have asked him to leave.

Oh, no. My dad was playing the long game. If I *had* been a witch and Dexter hadn't told me to duck, she would have hexed me while my back was turned. It would have been *me* who had to stay in a dark room for months instead of Head-master Krauss.

I could have kept up with reading assignments and homework, but this was college, not high school. Aside from history, almost all of my classes were practical work. I couldn't be graded in a lot of my classes if I wasn't present to do some kind of magic in front of my professor.

In other words, I most likely would have failed out of the Academy of the Profane if I had been a witch.

The board realized we had all these new superpowers and our brains hadn't finished developing yet, so they had a three strike policy. Azren couldn't expel Kaylee unless the board stepped in to override their policy, so she had two more opportunities to take out an innocent bystander trying to get rid of me.

So, it didn't matter Kaylee got online to find a super painful hex that most likely would have gotten me expelled and threw it while my back was turned and got her mom. The board was going to give her two more strikes.

Kaylee was probably going to flunk history on her own because she kept acting like Azren was lying about everything, but my dad was going to nudge that along faster by using the board's rules against them. Professors didn't have to let a student into class if they were late and most of them didn't.

My dad was just flunking her faster by declaring her late. She was the last person to get here, so he wasn't taking anyone down with her.

Three hands shot up as soon as my dad waved his hand and slammed the door behind her. They were all various minions. Legacy students who only got admitted because of their last name and were wasting this entire opportunity. They were here to find mates and get their trust fund.

Some of them were still sniffing around my idiot brother, even though he made it clear he was crazy about Dexter. And they didn't want Dexter in their coven if my brother was willing to give them the time of day, which he wasn't. Angels were created to love their god. Their god never intended for them to fall in love with anyone else and have babies. I didn't even know if angels were polyamorous. The other two angels I knew weren't. They were barking up the wrong tree.

"Excuse me, sir, but Kaylee wasn't late," Paris said.

"You can barely handle an eyeliner pencil, so I doubt you understand the vast concept of time like I do. Kaylee was late."

Dexter snorted a laugh and several people giggled. Paris was just as awful as Kaylee. She was probably the vice president of evil minions. Paris wasn't just nasty to Dexter and me. She referred to everyone who wasn't a legacy student as *the poors* and constantly acted like they were dirty and contaminated her precious air.

"You can't talk to me like that!" Paris shrieked.

"I can talk to you however the fuck I want. *You* on the other hand are eventually going to look those crooked raccoon eyes down at the wrong person and lose everything. And before you think you can talk to *me* or Azren a certain way, we could kill you with just a secondhand thought without stopping our lecture and then happily eat a sandwich while never thinking of you again. And before you say anything about the Paranormal Investigation Bureau and prison, they'd never find your body, and jail can't hold us. Consider your friend lucky she was only late. I saw the video."

Dexter started clapping. Kaylee had been awful to Dexter because he was trans. I didn't think Paris cared about that. Paris had looked down on Dexter because he wasn't rich, but she didn't start being terrible to him until he started dating my brother. Paris wanted an angel, so she was being a dick to Dexter.

And then Paris turned purple when most of the class started clapping because my dad just threatened to kill her for mouthing off. *The poors* in our history class were laughing at her, too. Paris grabbed her bag and stormed out of class.

My dad whirled around and waved his hand. A pack of Oreos appeared on everyone's desk. When my mom was tricked into bringing the God of Chaos back to this realm, he got obsessed with modern junk food. Oreos were his obsession for a long time. My dad still loved his cookies.

"That was dramatic. Anyway," my dad said, taking a bite out of his cookie.

Everyone tore into their cookies and my dad resumed his lecture like nothing happened. Maybe I *should* take the necklace off sooner than later.

Kaylee had two strikes left and Paris was egging her on. *That* was a lot more effective coming from a god than a witch.

REN

We needed a distraction. No one had turned up dead, but trying to figure out who did it the first time and stopping it from happening again was going really slowly because our two Fate-chosen didn't get along and the God of Death was being buried in all the administrative stuff that Headmaster Krauss had neglected.

It wasn't just the dodgeball team. There were supposed to be work-study assignments for people that needed the money and schedules to be rearranged for students with talent who had been picked for independent study. None of that had been done, so we'd hardly seen Azren.

I liked other people's drama, but not when I was involved. I needed Drake and George to get over everything and get along. I understood why Drake had his thing with witches, but he'd spent enough time around us to realize

George wasn't like that. George needed to get that Drake had some trauma he was working through.

Dodgeball tryouts were *perfect* for them to work through some shit. I didn't enjoy playing team sports and it wouldn't make their relationship perfect, but it would give them something to bond over. There would be fist bumping and chest hugs over goals. I'd watched Oscar do both with people he couldn't stand because they scored and the team won.

Church and I had already picked good seats at the dodgeball stadium. We weren't the only people who came to watch tryouts. There was a pretty decent crowd. Dodgeball had a huge following and all of the people intending to try out for cheerleading had come out for support.

West was missing. He was acting kind of shady before Church and I left. George was going to sign for Oscar on the field because West couldn't get super close to Oscar. West was like, a maniac when it came to dodgeball. He would have been out here if it was just Oscar. Watching his girlfriend play dodgeball? West should have been the first person out here.

When West finally showed up, I didn't know what the fuck he was doing. He was wearing a long trench coat, and it was completely buttoned up. Something didn't look right.

"Dude, are you naked under there?" Church asked.

West was definitely naked under that trench coat. That was weird even for West.

"Oscar, Drake, and George are *never* going to get picked unless I'm naked. This is a compromise."

Church shot me a horrified look. All it was going to take was West's trench coat popping open, and we were all going to see his dick. It was one thing when he was shifting, but dodgeball tryouts? There was a time and place for lion cock. This wasn't it.

"I don't even know what that means," I said.

"All you *need* to know is that if I don't watch dodgeball in the nude, shit gets bad. My team loses, players get injured, and one time a tornado called the game. My balls are blessed, man. Don't question the magic," West said, kissing my forehead. "I brought snacks."

West kissed a *lot* of guys for a straight dude. I'm not even sure Drake knew what hit him when West went for it. West pulled a massive bag of snacks from his trench coat and now the thirsty girls realized he was naked. They started giggling and trying to get his attention.

One of them walked over and West didn't even look up.

"Nope. I belong to that witch down there with legs for days," he said before she could speak. She huffed and stormed off.

"She could have wanted some chips," Church said.

"Trust me. She didn't," West said.

She definitely didn't.

"Look, they are starting," Church said. "Zion put Oscar, George, and Drake on the same team."

And George's massive angel brother. Dexter was on their team, too. I got why Michael and Dexter were a thing. They both had these amazing wings and people who *didn't* like Dexter were just weird to me. He was hilarious and brilliant.

The teams were set. Zion picked captains and Michael was the captain of Oscar's team. I got it. Not everyone knew sign language and Oscar never wanted to be captain. The Bell kids all knew it, so Michael could communicate with Oscar. There was a brief team huddle where everyone talked about what position they played and the captain decided if they were going to get it.

Michael wasn't an idiot and knew his shit. George took the forward position, Oscar was a center like usual, and Drake started putting on goalie gear.

Michael picked George as the team witch. The other team captain was a bear shifter and chose a warlock I didn't know. Zion had the box with the four elemental balls off to the side. When the game officially started, he opened it and the balls shot out.

George and the warlock would be fighting over which ball was the official one they'd be scoring with. Every team wanted the Earth ball. It wasn't as volatile as the other balls and slightly easier to tame. I had different opinions about that ball after it maimed my boyfriend.

The warlock went straight for the Earth ball, which was expected. George didn't try to fight him for it. I was used to seeing the team witch or warlocks fighting over the Earth balls. George went straight for the Air ball.

The rest of the team was trying to avoid getting smashed by the Fire and Water balls while the team witch did their things. The Air ball was an interesting choice. No one ever went for that one because it was easy to avoid and hard to tame. It could whip a player up in a cyclone and fling them off the field.

It mostly hung out in the air and took out the winged players, so the witches just ignored it. Plus, Oscar said the Air Ball was so hard to tame if a witch could get to it, it just wasted all this time, so it was never done.

"Why's she going for the Air Ball?" West asked. "Bold choice. That's kinky."

It kind of was. When the Air Ball noticed George was trying to tame it, it shot up in the air. She stretched her arms and Michael swooped down to pick her up and fly her in the air. Michael had these beautiful white-feathered wings. He beat them until they caught up with the Air Ball and George snagged it with her magic.

I couldn't believe what I was seeing. George tamed the fucking Air Ball before the warlock could get his Earth Ball under control. It was still shaking the ground under his feet. When she tossed the ball to Oscar, I *got* why she went for that one. Once the Air Ball was under the control of our team, you could tell it where to go and it would go there easier than their throwing it.

It zipped straight to Oscar, who took off running. The other team's Fire ball tried to take him out, so he dove out of the way and tossed it to Dexter. Dexter was *fantastic* in the air. He beat his wings and got nearly halfway across the field before a witch tried to manipulate the Water Ball at him.

Dexter did a back flip and heaved his ball at a succubus. She took it all the way to the goal, distracted their goalie with some sex vibes, and made the shot.

West stood up and shrieked. He grabbed Church, and me and yanked us into a group hug.

"Holy shit! Did you see that? Our girlfriend tamed the fucking *Air Ball.* I'm going to vigorously fuck her after she makes the team. I'm not even going to let her shower first because I want that sweat on me. It'll probably make me point zero five percent better at dodgeball by osmosis."

"That's gross, West. Shower with her and wash the sweat and dodgeball dirt off of her. It's what I do with Oscar. She'll appreciate that a lot more than you getting horny when she feels gross."

"I'll bet our girl is totally into freaky and nasty. Do you

think she'd be into doing it on the dodgeball field once everyone has cleared out?"

"Too soon, West. Someone was murdered out there and we don't know who did it," Church said.

It must be some kind of day if Church was the sane one when it came to sex with George. Don't get me wrong, she was fantastic in bed, especially with the connection she had with Oscar and me. West and Church were slightly deranged when it came to our girlfriend.

"Oh, shit, look! We're going to get to see Baby Drake in action!" West yelled.

I adored West. He was one of us. We'd never try to tame or change him. His balls being celestially blessed and could affect the outcome of a dodgeball match wasn't even that weird. Some of Oscar's teammates in high school had some pretty gross pregame rituals that made being in the same room with them pretty stinky.

He coined the nickname Baby Drake and nothing about that made sense. I didn't know if Drake was bisexual, but he was definitely hot. He had this dark-ginger bad boy thing going. Drake had the tortured past, and he was also a musician who was willing to help Oscar. He also knew sign language. Like, *I'd* be into bringing Drake into a relationship with Oscar and me if he could be a little more open-minded about witches, but we were with George and those two didn't get along at all.

There was nothing soft and baby-like about Drake.

Like, he was guarding the goal like he was fully prepared to kill someone before he let the Earth Ball get by him. Some of the players on the other team weren't very good. They were concentrating more on dodging the balls flying at them than being open to catch the Earth Ball and score for their team. A good dodgeball player had to be able to do both.

The bear shifter Zion had chosen as team captain and the warlock he chose to tame the team ball were doing most of the work. They were good players. Good enough to make the final cut when the rest of their team wasn't up to par. They were showboating pretty hard, too.

The only person who could stop them from scoring at this point was Drake. The bear shifter thought he had it and he got arrogant about it. He was trying to show off. I guess he thought he needed to make a big impression after what George and Michael did in the air and his team was already down one point.

He made one key error. He tried to look Drake in the eyes in a show of bravado. Drake snared him right away, and he froze. Before his warlock friend could get to him and rescue the Earth Ball and try to score, the Water Ball hit him with a tidal wave and washed him halfway across the field.

Drake gave this dark sexy grin, picked up the Earth Ball, and threw it straight to the closest player on his team. Which happened to be George. She also smiled when she caught and tried to bean the warlock in the head with it. Drake whooped when it slammed into his chest so hard, he dropped it instead of catching it.

So, those two *could* get along and support each other when it came to sports. It was a fucking start.

GEORGE

I missed playing dodgeball with my idiot brother. I thought those days were over when he graduated high school because the Academy of the Profane didn't have a team. I had several tricks I couldn't do without him because he had those wings that I'd never tell him were fabulous because he had a fat head about them.

My team won. The other team had some good people, but they were no match for us. I scored the last goal with an assist from Dexter, who was a beast in the air. Dexter was closest to me and tackled me. The rest of my team puppy piled on me.

This is what I loved about dodgeball. This match didn't even matter. It was a tryout and Zion was watching how we played. There would be people from the losing team who made the cut and people from my team who didn't. But we were just so excited we won, anyway.

We were all sweaty, and dirty, and some of us were

burned or bleeding. That was dodgeball. Zion stepped on the field with his clipboard.

"That was a good show. I think I can not only put together a good team with this, but we're going to kick some ass. I'll be posting the final list on the academy message board as soon as I can get Azren to show me how to fucking do that and I finalize the team. Which is already making me cranky because back in my day, you had to drive to the stadium and read your name off a fucking list and now I have to figure out idiot message boards because your generation is all about instant gratification. Anyway, go take a fucking shower. All those hormones mean you're also extra stinky after a match and as a bear shifter, some of you are pretty offensive right now. Get out of here."

Zion Skinner just called us all entitled children who reeked, and I was *still*-ass crazy excited that I just tried out for his dodgeball team. I was getting ready to leave when Dexter pulled me off to the side.

"Dude, my brother said he first noticed you in flying class and I see why."

"That's what I want to talk to you about. Michael told me your secret. I want to go flying with Michael and I want to play dodgeball. I'm better in the air on the dodgeball team. I can't fly and bind my chest at the same time. I can't be *me* and a pixie at the same time right now and I can't afford top surgery. I won't be able to for a while. Michael said you might be able to do something like that with no healing time."

"I'm pretty sure I *can*, but I've never done anything that big before. I've mostly only made sure my sister's manicure is always perfect. I'm going to have to ask Azren for tips. They are tutoring me. Just let me make sure I can actually do this before I try."

"Thanks. I think your fan club is waiting and so is mine."

Michael scooped Dexter up like a caveman and carried him off the field on his shoulders. My guys were waiting for me. West was suspiciously in a trench coat that I was pretty sure he was naked underneath.

Drake was with them and he was grinning. I'd give it to Drake. We couldn't get through an entire meal in the dining hall without him getting in at least one dig at me, but we played dodgeball together seamlessly. He was getting slightly better about being rude to me, but I still had no idea what I was supposed to be helping him with.

"Bold move taming the Air Ball. I've literally never seen that done before," Drake said.

"Me neither," Oscar said.

"That's because no one does it," West said. "I've watched old dodgeball games from way back and everyone goes for the Earth ball or tries to take the Fire Ball out of commission."

"They should," Oscar said. "Passing it or scoring with it is *so* much easier than any of the other balls. The Earth Ball is bulky and vibrates. The Fire Ball won't burn you once it's been tamed, but it's still hot and it shocks you. You can drop them if you aren't careful. The Air Ball is light and I've never played an easier game."

"Have you tried the Water Ball?" Drake asked. "Something tells me you did, but you decided to make the Air Ball your signature move."

Was that a compliment? I was having a blast trying to make the dodgeball team doing moves I perfected with my brother on the lawn outside the Library of the Profane. I wasn't trying to impress Drake, but if he could be pleasant right now, so could I.

"You can tame the Water Ball, but it's pointless. You have to make it solid to be able to play dodgeball with it. It becomes too cold to hold for very long and insanely slippery. My parents are huge dodgeball fans. My dad, Felix, got all the kids a set of balls for Yule one year.

"Michael and I spent ages figuring out tricks and experimenting with the different balls. Michael's god never intended angels to reproduce, meaning there was never a failsafe so Michael would get his magic when he turned eighteen. He had his wings, and I had magic, so we played a lot of dodgeball while my parents and siblings cheered us on."

Drake's whole demeanor changed. It was like me having a happy childhood and supportive parents pissed him off. I didn't even know what his deal was because as soon as I thought we were making progress and I'd actually find out, Drake would flip a switch and go back to hating me.

My dads had a whole-ass game plan because every woman in my house had our periods synced as soon as someone got old enough to get theirs and Matilda and I were pretty dramatic about them between the ages of thirteen and sixteen.

Drake's mood swings were worse than mine when I was still ranting about the unfairness of having to deal with periods for eternity since I was immortal and would eventually stop aging. It was kind of a bitch that I had cosmic powers and still had to deal with cramps.

I was a little asshole about that for a while. Kind of like Drake.

"I need a shower," I announced.

I was sweaty, dirty, and I had werewolf's blood on my shirt because he tried to dodge the Water Ball and broke his nose on my clavicle. We only had one broken nose and since my signature move was taming the Air Ball, no one got yeeted off the field by a cyclone. Overall, it was a successful game.

Drake wasn't going to ruin that for me.

GEORGE

West heard 'shower' and immediately tried to kidnap me back to my dorm. I wasn't going to say no to that. West was the type of guy who would be supportive of anything. I could have been terrible at dodgeball and West would have told me I was the best person out there and called *the* Zion Skinner an ass-face for not letting me on the team.

The fact that I *wasn't* terrible at dodgeball probably had West all horny and honestly, so was I. Winning games was sexy. The only reason I didn't have a lot more sex after games in high school was that everyone knew my brother and they were still scared he would beat their ass for defiling his sister even after he graduated.

I just had one question.

"Why are you wearing nothing but a trench coat?"

"You play dodgeball, so you'll *get* it. If I watch dodgeball with clothes on, something goes wrong for my team. I can't curse or hex like a witch, but if I'm not free balling during a dodgeball, it's like my team is cursed."

"Your balls *are* pretty fabulous."

"I know, right? Some thirsty siren came over when she realized she might get a peek at all of this, but I sent her away. I get that you're a strong, secure utter goddess in many ways, but it would boost my ego if you started a slap fight and pulled her hair if she stares too hard when I'm naked in magical combat."

"You heard Matilda. Our parents taught us how to finish it, not pull hair."

"Can you at least pretend to be irrationally angry about it?"

"I am! We had sex in front of the whole school at the moon and it's pretty obvious I licked you and claimed you. Is nothing sacred to these bitches? You were out there half naked for *science*. Who was she? Maybe I do want to pull her hair a little."

"Thank you."

"Oh, I didn't say that to stroke your ego. I marinated on it for two seconds and I really am mad about it. You're the first guy I've ever met who hit on me because of *me* and not my dad."

"Now that I've met your dad, he's cool and everything, but he does nothing for me sexually. I don't need a big cosmic favor. I need someone who thinks I'm awesome and is also awesome. I need someone who laughs at my silly jokes and doesn't act weird around Oscar. I need *you*. I don't care what you and your dad are."

West was my ride or die who just got me. Nothing changed for him when he figured out my secret. And my secret could have been something really awful and West wouldn't have given a shit. I hoped the rest of them reacted the same when I told them.

But for now, I was back in my dorm and West had already taken his trench coat off. There wasn't any cross over with human and supernatural sports, but humans had pregame rituals and things they thought brought their teams luck. And most of them had a history of getting violent when they saw real magic after a certain time in history.

I'd also been watching and playing dodgeball since I was a kid. There were things I *had* to do before a game or things went to shit. West looked insanely good naked. His balls probably *were* lucky. I mean, I had an amazing time with them at the moon orgy and I was pretty sure I was about to get to play with them again.

"Having furious sex after winning a dodgeball game has always been on my bucket list, but my idiot brother cock-blocked me."

"I'm pretty sure your idiot brother is getting topped by a pixie right now."

I covered my ears and started singing.

"Anything involving my brother having sex is my no-no place and you're ruining the fact that you're naked and sexy in my dorm and I have you to myself."

"Well, I *was* going to ravage you on the dodgeball field because I was pretty sure getting your sweat on me would make me a little better at dodgeball. Ren said washing you in the shower was more civilized."

Oh, shit. New kink unlocked.

I stepped in and yanked West to me so I could kiss him.

"We can do that, too, later."

"Come here, you," West growled, scooping me up.

He carried me to the bathroom and started stripping

my sweaty, dirty clothes off of me. West licked me from between my breasts all the way to my forehead. I laughed and pushed him away.

"Just in case all your dodgeball sweat and grime is blessed."

"It doesn't work like that."

"Nothing about dodgeball makes sense. Get that sexy body in the shower."

The Academy of the Profane was built before indoor plumbing. They could have done shared bathrooms and communal showers when they decided to upgrade from chamber pots and well-water baths, but the people who donated a ton of money and sent their kids here didn't want that. So, they made the dorm rooms smaller to fit a clawfoot tub, then eventually fitted showerheads.

I wasn't complaining. I had plenty of room to have my wicked way with West, even if he wanted to get a little rough. I conjured a non-slip mat for the tub the first night here because I didn't want Mags or Matilda getting hurt and I didn't want to demolish something if I slipped. Lindsay Krauss was the kind of bitch who would expel me for destroying school property for falling in the bathtub.

West was absolutely adorable. He was intent on washing the sweat and grime off of me. It rained two days before dodgeball tryouts. The field was playable but muddy. It was even in my hair. West was going to scrub it all out. I tried to grab him again to get him to kiss me, but he just swatted at my hands.

"No touching. You're filthy."

"I thought my filth was blessed."

"I did. And I licked it for science. Azren and I are the only people not related to you that know your secret. Azren has to be all private about it and is going to treat you like an equal. I still don't know why you let everyone think you're a witch and I'm not going to ask, but I want to treat you like a god. Let me worship this beautiful body and wash you after you played a badass dodgeball game."

I'd been able to bathe myself for a while now, but it was kind of nice to let West do it.

"Lilith showed up in my delivery room with my necklace just in case one of us ended up a god. Back when gods were more common, some of them looked down on born gods. They thought we were different and more dangerous than gods who were created from nothing.

"There's not a lot of them on this realm anymore, but the necklace was to protect me and let me have a normal childhood until I could defend myself. I technically *could* have taken it off in high school, but every god has a job or a specific power and I didn't know mine.

"Azren helped me figure that out, but it paints an entirely different target on my back. Apparently, my big superpower is that I can mimic anyone nearby. So, instead of faking witchcraft like I thought I'd been doing, I'm actually *doing* it. A lot of gods consider themselves special snowflakes so they aren't going to like it I can mimic their magic. And apparently, gods can die."

"Are you serious?" West shrieked, yanking me to his chest. "So, you could actually *be* a lioness just by standing next to me and do all the fun things lions do when they are shifted? We could *totally* stalk Kaylee and make her run unless she wants to get pounced. It would be epic."

West was the first person I told all of that who wasn't related to me or Azren. His reaction was perfect and I couldn't stop laughing.

"Could you imagine Kaylee not being able to walk

through campus without being paranoid about getting pounced on by two lions? That would be amazing."

"Paris, too, because she's also a dick. I know you're a god and everything, but can I ask you a huge favor?"

"Anything."

"Can you wash my hair?"

Oh, shit. A lion asking someone to wash their hair was a *huge* step. You *never* touched their mane unless they asked you to. You had to earn that right. A lion never invited someone to care for their mane unless they were feeling the mate pull. And West looked terrified because I wasn't a shifter who felt the whole mate thing. If I refused, I was essentially rejecting him.

I said I was doing the whole college thing instead of traveling the world and learning from other gods because I wanted the same experiences my mom and aunt had. Neither of them formed their covens in college. They learned, played the field, and had fun. I also wasn't one of those girls who was only here to meet men.

But then I met them. And I wanted to keep all of them. West was so insanely perfect, I'd happily play with his hair until he fell asleep. I grabbed West and kissed him.

"I'd be fucking *honored* to care for your mane."

WEST

My dad said I would know when I met the person or persons I wanted to let touch my hair. I knew when I met her she was going to be as cool as my five moms and just an amazing person. And she was. George was everything I ever wanted in a mate and several things I didn't know until I met her.

I was going to wait to ask her, but I just blurted it out in the shower. I'd never been turned down by a single girl in my life. If I got caught by an authority figure, a rakish smile and mane toss usually got me out of it. Older women had been hitting on me since I was fifteen.

None of them were gods. I didn't give a shit that she was. I thought it was pretty fucking cool. It was even cooler she was a mimic and could do lion things with me. I knew she *liked* me and she didn't seem to look down on anyone because they weren't a god. We were having a ton of fun, but I didn't know if she wanted a group thing with gods.

And then she said yes. She wanted me, too, and it was just the best feeling in the world. My dad tried to explain it to the kids because he did this five times, but Pops barely graduated high school and wasn't good with fancy words. We got the gist of it, but it felt better than I ever imagined.

"Okay, so as soon you recommended those products for curly hair, I ordered them. You just washed my hair with it. I don't have the top-secret exclusive-lion stuff and I don't want to get this wrong and fuck up your fabulous mane."

I knew she ordered the stuff I recommended before I even set foot in her shower because there were a few things on this earth I was good at and haircare was one of them. Her curls had been *banging* lately, even when she didn't feel like dealing with her hair and threw it up in a messy ponytail.

I leaned in just in case some perverted ghost was spying on us. Bethany was popping out of random places to assault Church's nuts. George and I looked *really* good naked. Someone could be peeking, trying to get the top-secret lion knowledge I was about to drop.

"The shampoo and conditioner you got is the exact same stuff that is exclusive to lions, minus certain potions for shine and to stimulate the follicles. It's not going to damage my hair to wash it without the potion."

George let out the breath she was holding.

"Oh, good because this is a big thing for me and I really don't want to fuck this up."

And there went my ego, swelling to epic proportions. My lioness had insane cosmic powers, and I just watched her be a total badass on the dodgeball field, but this was a big deal to her. It wasn't just her words. It was her body language and scent. This meant just as much to her as it did to me.

And it was perfect. She washed and conditioned my mane just right. George scratched my scalp and worked the conditioner through my ends. She combed my hair out with her fingers then gently directed me under the water to rinse.

Bastet created lion shifters, and I fired off a little prayer thanking her because George wasn't content to just wash my mane. She was on her knees with my cock down her throat and my balls in her palm.

Ah, fuck. She just tamed the fucking *Air* Ball, scored a ton of goals, and beaned a couple of people in the face who missed the entire point of *dodge*ball. It was sexy as fuck and she just accepted me as her mate. I should be the one on my knees with my face buried between those muscular thighs.

Should I take my dick out of her mouth and show her what an utter goddess she was on the dodgeball field? Because she was really good at this and seemed into it. I started purring as soon as she started washing my hair, but now it was rumbling in my chest. I kept trying to repeat what my Pops told me. Lions *do not* make biscuits on a girl's head when she's sucking his dick. It just felt so fucking good.

George did this little trick with her throat and tongue while massaging my balls and I was a goner. And I was totally making biscuits on her head because I was a fucking lion and that's what we did when we felt good.

Then she snaked her hand behind me and stuck her finger up my ass. No one had ever done that to me before and I wasn't even mad about it because I came harder than I ever had in my life. I threw back my head and let out a total King of the Jungle roar.

Let *everyone* in Sigmis dorm know I'd just had a record-breaking orgasm. Damn. I was a little verklempt and my knees were shaky. It was *that* good. I turned the water off and guided her out of the shower.

I *fully* intended on returning the favor and utterly ravaging my mate.

DRAKE

I finally had a group of friends at the Academy of the Profane, but I *hated* who I was becoming. I could hear myself being rude to George and I couldn't stop myself. I'd long figured out she wasn't interested in anything involving magic with Basilisk parts and really did just want to stop the murders and help me with my shit.

George was funny and kind of awkward considering her dad was a god and she was the strongest witch in this school. So, what was my fucking problem? It wasn't even that she was a witch.

I was jealous of her family because I never had that. My adoptive mother was amazing. I loved her and she gave me a great life. Azren stepped in and made it better. I had a great childhood. I never wanted for anything. And I was irrationally pissed off that I was even questioning that for a minute because she got to grow up with her birth family who seemed to be utterly perfect.

That was totally my issue and not hers. I wouldn't have wished what happened to me on anyone. I needed to make it right because I hated myself every time I blurted out something terrible to her.

She'd only used words against me so far and they weren't even that harsh. George had endless patience. She hadn't hexed me or anything. And even if I wasn't suspicious of witches, she probably should have by now because I was being awful.

I didn't want to lose this group of friends. West, Oscar, Ren, and Church were amazing. I even liked her twin and her girlfriends, even if one of them was a witch. I could tell they were trying to facilitate some kind of truce here because of fate and I was the one ruining everything.

"Can I talk to you? Alone?" I asked after dinner. "We can go to my dorm room. My roommate is super into this bear shifter because she throws him around. He won't be there."

"Not worried I'm going to steal your toenails?" George asked.

I deserved that, but Mags just shot her some epic stink eye and tsked her. George immediately apologized. I didn't get it. Mags started later than the rest of us, but she seemed to know the twins. She was dating Matilda, but George seemed to listen to her a lot considering she was her sister's girlfriend.

"No, that was fair," I said. "I know you're not going to steal my stuff."

"Well, thanks. I guess."

She followed me to my dorm and took a seat at my roommate's desk. I sat on my bed and sighed. This would be easier if I could play my violin first. Everything was easier with music and I *still* hadn't figured out the ending of my piece.

"So, I'm sorry how I've been acting. It's not just what witches did to Basilisks that made me distrust them. Someone murdered my parents in front of me when I was a baby. A reaper from Azren's realm raised me with a little help from Azren. I was always certain it was witches who killed my parents, but now I don't know what I think.

"You're amazing and I'm not even upset with you. I'm taking something out on you that isn't even your fault. You have amazing parents and every time you talk about them, I think about how mine were murdered. And it's stupid because my adoptive mother was loving, kind, and went above and beyond. It's not even rational, but I keep doing it."

George didn't say anything, and I didn't know what she was thinking. She got up and walked over to my bed.

"Lay down and scooch."

I did what she asked, but I definitely didn't know what she wanted until she laid down and snuggled with me. I tensed at first, but then I relaxed. This was nice, and she smelled amazing.

"I'm supposed to be helping you find out who killed your parents, aren't I?"

"Yeah, but I think it's connected to why my mom left the Academy of the Profane before she could graduate. I asked Oscar to help me with the ghosts, but Bethany refused to tell me. I'm in my mom's old dorm room and I found a box that I think was hers, but there's a blood lock on it. Azren says they can break it, but I think it should be my blood that opens it if it was hers. I'm just not ready to find out it might not be."

And she squeezed me. She'd been great, and she was *holding* me right now when I'd been nothing but nasty to her.

"So, take your time. Between you, me, Azren, and everyone else, we can start looking into your mom now that we're all on the same page. And maybe you should meet the rest of my family. Everyone is going to the library for dinner on Friday, even Azren. You'll see we aren't perfect. We're loud, messy, and my dad Balthazar is probably going to get glitter all over my dad Felix for no reason other than it pisses him off. He's been doing that for nineteen years and it never gets old to him.

"My aunt will be there with Loki and Freya. I don't know if my parents invited Lilith and Lucifer. It's a get-together with my college friends and fate made you one of us. I get it and I can get over you kind of being a dick to me."

"'Kind of?'"

"Okay, you were a massive dick, but it was just *words*. You snipped at me. It's not like you started a whole-ass campaign and have been trying to get me expelled. And you didn't throw a hex at my back."

Kaylee Krauss. Yeah, I guess compared to her, I had been an angel. Though, I'd now met an angel, and he was kind of growly and possessive about his boyfriend. I didn't know what that guy had done to Dexter, but Michael beat the shit out of him and tossed him halfway across the dining hall.

I heard them all bad mouthing her and I joined in, but I never found out what the real story was. I had just assumed it was a witch pissing contest, so I asked.

The actual story sounded too ridiculous to be true. You couldn't sue a minor on Azren's realm. It was *wild* it was even allowed on this one. I got that Minerva left a lot of stuff to George in her will, but her parents would be controlling all of that until she was eighteen. I knew who Minerva Krauss was, too. Azren spoke fondly of her and a lot of reapers respected her work in curse breaking because it saved lives and made their jobs easier. My adoptive mom had several of her books and had gone to hear her talk several times.

"The reapers on Azren's realm loved her. They'd travel through the veil to this realm when she released a new book and they loved getting them signed and hearing her speak."

"She would have loved that. Everyone remembers her as this brilliant witch who was a spinster, but she brought the filthiest books to the book club she was in with my mom and aunt. Like, my mom likes her smut and has five husbands and my aunt is handfasted to Loki, who has got up to shit in all kinds of genders and sometimes animals. Some of the books she brought were almost too dirty for them. My mom always encouraged us to read, but Matilda and I couldn't join her book club while Minerva was suggesting books."

"She sounds like a hell of a woman. Ketura raised me and Azren was always around. They all had amazing things to say about her."

"Drake Nathara, did you just say something nice about a witch? I might die from shock. I seriously am. I'm literally dying from shock!"

George pretended to convulse and fell right off my bed onto the floor. She popped right up and tossed her hair over her shoulder.

"I'm a dodgeball player. I *know* how to fall."

She was also an adorable shade of purple because she was embarrassed. The strongest witch in this entire school just fell out of my bed being silly and now she was awkwardly worried I was going to make fun of her for it. I could literally *feel* the power coming off of her, but I couldn't believe I ever thought she was a threat.

"I didn't grow up in a realm with witches and I'm still not sure one of them didn't murder my parents, but now that I've met you, I'm willing to admit that not all witches are bad. Because girl, you could probably destroy this entire school and we're probably going to win a ton of dodgeball games because of you, but you aren't threatening at all."

George threw my pillow at my face.

"You've said a lot of rude things to me, but that was the meanest."

"I was actually trying to be nice right then."

"You aren't very good at it," George laughed.

"You don't strike me as someone who needs their ass kissed. Besides, West and Church do that *a lot.*"

"West is my ride or die and Church is my stalker."

"That's never going to be me, but I can be civil. I *will* give you a hard time about stupid shit that doesn't matter and you can call me an asshole."

"I can accept that. I need someone who calls me on my shit that isn't my twin or Mags. But you're coming to dinner with my family and if you try to hide, I know three gods who can find you and poof you there. And I'll twist your arm. You played dodgeball with my brother. I grew up brawling with him. Don't make me fuck up your hands. It would be a crime if you had to stop playing the violin and we need you on goalie if we going to win dodgeball games. You're coming to dinner," George said, leaving my door.

So, she was also bossy as fuck. I felt better. I finally told her the truth, and I finally felt a little more comfortable with all the witches around campus. I actually liked George, and I liked the people she kept around her. It was great having friends here and they could help me get answers about my parents and stop a murderer.

And now that I'd made my peace with her, my writer's block had finally lifted. I knew *exactly* how to finish my piece.

GEORGE

I felt better after talking to Drake. He was definitely awful to me, but I understood him now. Drake would have been a different person if his parents hadn't been murdered. His reaction to me wouldn't have been so extreme if he had grown up around witches. His first experience with them was coming to the Academy of the Profane.

I could have made him grovel, but why? He wasn't as rude to me as Kaylee and her crew were and we needed to be on the same page because there was a murderer out there. Drake needed closure, too. And I had a feeling fate threw us together because the answers to both questions were either the same or closely related.

And if Drake was going to be civilized, so could I. Drake didn't just need to find out about his parents. I wasn't even a witch, but Drake needed friends in this realm and to see not all witches wanted to murder him. Which meant I needed to introduce him to Bell women who were actually witches.

But I was still a hot mess. I *knew* I was good at dodgeball. I played a good game. But it had been almost a week and Zion hadn't posted the team roster yet. If we asked him about it in magical combat, he'd rant about my generation and message boards.

Azren said they showed Zion how to make an account and post it, but he kept forgetting his password and locking his account out. By the time it unlocked, he had forgotten how to use the message board. Azren offered to post the list, but bear shifters were the *most* stubborn of all supernatural races and he was *going* to make this work.

Even though we were all hot messes and hitting refresh on the message board.

West wasn't even a student here, and he was hitting refresh. We were at lunch and we were supposed to have dinner at my parents' tonight. Ren was doom scrolling on his phone while everyone was finishing up. Ren had given me a single earring he stole this morning. He did that a lot. Sometimes, he stole the matching earring later, but I had a ton of mismatched jewelry his klepto fox had stolen for me.

"Dodgeball team is posted," Ren yelled for the entire dining hall to hear.

Mags snatched her phone up.

"I'll have you know that they were waiting to post the cheerleading team in solidarity with the dodgeball team. It's about fucking time."

"I *know* Matilda made it," Mina said.

Mina had it bad for my sister and I loved everything about it. Mina was good for her.

"Damn. I was hoping Belladonna Mortem didn't make

it, but she's annoyingly good at cheerleading and, apparently, my co-captain," Matilda moaned.

"She's terrible. If you need me to fuck with her, we can be besties," Church said, patting my sister's hand.

"I can't look. Someone tell me if I made it."

"You made it," Drake said. "You're team witch. Your brother is the team captain. Dexter, Oscar, and I made it, too. You can look now and see who's on the team."

"Thanks. You don't suck today."

"It's still early, witch."

I stuck my tongue out at Drake. Now that we made our peace, he was pretty funny. Our relationship was growing into one where we poked at each other, but didn't mean it. Also, earlier this week, Drake gave us a concert while Oscar had his hands on his violin. I could tell Oscar could feel the music because a tear ran down his cheek as Drake played because Drake was that good.

Drake was good people. He just needed to get over some shit.

I looked over at my brother and several people who had tried out with us were standing around his table. Before we could get up to join, Belladonna Mortem came over to our table.

It was a pity she was such vampire supremacist bitch because she was almost grotesquely gorgeous. She was so perfect, you either stared too much or it was hard to look at her. Vampires were naturally beautiful since they were predators, but Belladonna had naturally-white blonde hair, ice-blue eyes, and that supernatural glow that parasitic races had when they were well fed.

I wasn't going to do a damned thing to her because she'd only shoulder checked me once and told me I wasn't good enough for Church, but a big-ass zit on that perfect face would make me feel better. If she escalated, I would.

I felt bad for Belladonna if she tried to start shit with Matilda. My sister didn't need a god for a dad and a twin. She would *destroy* Belladonna Mortem. She had Mags, Mina, and Church all willing to do her bidding. Matilda didn't do minions. She had friends, girlfriends, and family she was fiercely devoted to who. had her back because she was a good person.

Belladonna ignored me and scowled at Church.

"You need to come to your senses and stop slumming it before you end up looking totally ridiculous. Anyway, you and I are going to be co-captains. If I *have* to share the cheerleading team with anyone, you were the most adequate choice out of everyone who tried out. I have several good ideas for the direction of the team that I'd prefer you not get all shifter and fight me about."

Oh, my fuck. This girl right here. No one talked like that anymore. People stopped pretending other supernaturals were inferior because of what they were a long time ago because everyone had good and bad traits they got from their gods.

And some of it was straight-up lies. Shifters weren't inherently violent and prone to fights. That was propaganda started *ages* ago when a wolf shifter became more popular than a really inefficient king who taxed his people unfairly and used their taxes to buy himself luxuries. Everyone knew that. They taught it in high school history, but you still had idiots like Belladonna who still repeated it.

"Look, I'm going to level with you," Matilda said. "You're a decent cheerleader, but if you think you can talk to me and anyone who isn't a vampire like that, I will destroy you. There are more of us on the cheerleading team than there are vampires with shitty beliefs like yours. I will overthrow you harder than a basket toss and no one will be around to catch you. Don't fuck with me. I have ideas, too."

Belladonna didn't look angry, and she didn't pitch a fit. Kaylee would have. She almost looked like she...respected Matilda and was a little intrigued.

"I want this team to be the best. Can we talk?"

"If you stop being racist against everyone who isn't a vampire."

"You good?" I asked.

"I can handle it," Matilda said.

She could. Matilda handled her shit much better than I did. We all got up to join the other dodgeball players at my brother's table. The bear shifter who was team captain of the other team and the warlock he chose for the team witch had made the team. The bear shifter wasn't a freshman, but he introduced himself as Innis and scooped me up to sit on his shoulder.

"We are going to *beat the shit* out of everyone in the league between all of us and a team witch that can do *that* to an Air Ball. It wanted nothing to do with my team. We couldn't even intercept it," Innis said, smacking the shit out of my thigh like I was a show pony.

Dodgeball guys were great. Most of them weren't threatened by women at all. If you proved yourself on the field, you either became their little sister or they forgot you had a vagina. I was pretty sure I was just another dude to Innis, but my idiot brother was scowling at him.

"She's also my little sister and you're manhandling her."

"I'm manhandling her *respectfully* like her very gay teammate. I'm not into girls at all."

"And if he wasn't manhandling me respectfully, I could handle it myself, butthole."

"You're all going to lose if *she's* on the team," Kaylee sneered as she stopped by our table.

"Seriously," Paris laughed. "God genes have to be insanely potent and she ended up a dud. That old bear shifter they roped into coaching dodgeball must not have any idea what he's doing. They should have brought in an actual coach instead of letting a teacher do it."

An entire team of insanely strong dodgeball players stopped everything to look at those two. Kaylee and Paris also just drew the attention of the entire cheerleading squad. Neither of them tried out for cheerleading or came out to watch dodgeball tryouts like a good bit of the student body did. The people who tried out for cheerleading came to watch the dodgeball team and everyone who tried out for dodgeball came out to support the cheerleaders. And a good bit of people who were trying out for neither came out for both.

Anyone with half a brain knew Zion Skinner wasn't some rando they just asked to coach dodgeball. He was one of the best players in the league back in his day. Zion led his team to countless world champions. He retired before anyone at this academy was born, but anyone who knew dodgeball knew who he was because he was *that* famous.

"Excuse you, but did you just insult our team witch whose signature move is taming the Air Ball *and* Zion Skinner? Are your parents siblings or did they just drop you on your head? I can't imagine any other reason you'd be *that* stupid. You have to be a legacy student because there's no way in hell you got into the Academy of the Profane on your test scores," Innis growled.

The entire dodgeball team started throwing shade at

Kaylee and Paris and then the cheerleaders joined in. And they all had experience with verbal barbs on the field that sometimes escalated to actual brawls. Even the cheerleaders got into fistfights sometimes. Kaylee and Paris had never started shit with an entire dodgeball team before, but it looked like they just did. The cheerleaders weren't all that fond of them, either. Some of that was Matilda, but surprisingly, a lot of it was Belladonna.

I had my siblings, familiar, and my guys who would always have my back, but it looked like the dodgeball team and the cheerleading squad had it, too.

DRAKE

I hadn't applied for a library card at the Library of the Profane, even though it wasn't that far from the academy. I wanted one. It was pretty famous even in Azren's realm. I *wanted* a library card. The system only got snippy if you were going to abuse the contents, which I wasn't. Getting declined for a library card sounded traumatic and horrifically embarrassing, so I didn't.

This was supposed to be some meet the boyfriends and girlfriends dinner. George was bringing West, Oscar, Church, and Ren. Michael had invited Dexter and Matilda was bringing Mina and Mags. I was starting to feel like one of them. I liked how George and I had settled into giving each other a hard time.

But I wasn't dating her.

It was *weird* being invited to the meet the boyfriend dinner and she pretty much threatened to have me celestially kidnapped if I said no. Azren probably wouldn't, but I'd been sitting through her dad's history classes and he was totally devoted to his kids. He'd been kicking Kaylee Krauss out of class for tardiness since he started teaching, even when she got there before he did.

Bless Paris, she'd been trying to stick up for her friend and Reyson was destroying her in front of the entire class. She usually stormed out. All over that video Dexter posted and Kaylee's history with George. And I was pretty sure Reyson knew how Paris was treating Dexter because he was very vicious.

Azren wouldn't hunt me like a wounded animal and kidnap me to the library, but if George told Reyson she really wanted me there, her daddy totally would.

So, I was currently outside the Library of the Profane with everyone like I was a boyfriend.

The library was massive and imposing and there were three gods on the front steps. I knew Azren and Reyson. The redhead who looked like a seven-foot-tall adult Peter Pan and that he was absolutely going to give every single boyfriend and girlfriend here a hard time had to be Loki.

There were two women who were identical twins. One of them had to be George's mom because George and Matilda looked just like them. One wore her hair in waves and the other had hers dyed red.

The witch with the black, curly hair was George's mom. She introduced herself as Ripley and then introduced everyone else. Ripley was a hugger. She hugged all of us even me. And she squeezed me tight like she was happy to meet me and I actually was a boyfriend.

"So, I'm sure you're all wonderful or my daughter wouldn't be dating you and two of my husbands would have ratted you out since they are teachers at the academy. I *could* take you straight up to the living quarters, but that's not the kind of momma bear I am. Your first test of the night is going to be applying for a library card."

"I've already done my tests," Balthazar said. "None of you have anything nasty on your hard drives and your browser history isn't super weird."

What.the.fuck?

"I'm not a boyfriend," I pointed out.

All the parents just started laughing like they knew something I didn't.

"Oh, sweetie," Ripley said. "Maybe not *now*, but fate is meddling with you. Besides, Reyson has been translating a lot of our old diaries. There was a family of Basilisks that ruled the Persian Empire for several centuries. We have several diaries from their monarchs that Reyson translated and Felix formatted and converted to eBook form. You can't check them out without a library card. So, get your ass inside and bleed for me."

Did George's mom just smack me on the ass?

The inside of the library was gorgeous. We walked through the lobby to the front desk. There was an ornate bowl in the center. Ripley pulled out a jeweled athame.

"I know there are three gods here, but it only takes a drop. There's no need to be macho and slash your palm. I will judge if you bleed on my desk. It's an antique."

"Just do it," Bram whispered to us.

"I'll go first," Mina said.

Of course, she would. Mina was pretty bold. She went first until it was just me. Everyone got approved for their library card. George's dad Felix was standing behind me.

"It's nothing. Fate wouldn't have pushed you toward our kid if the library was going to deny you. I think you'll really like those diaries," Felix said.

"They sound fascinating."

"Oh, they are. I've already read them. There was a Basilisk queen in that era who was fierce and powerful. I think you'll like her diary."

"I thought you couldn't leave with books," I said.

"For a while, you couldn't," Balthazar said.

"Ripley started getting together with other magical libraries and translating books that don't have dangerous knowledge. We're making them available in eBook form so people can borrow books from other libraries. My wife knows a lot of these books are dangerous and not everyone should have access to them, but Ripley also knows books have power and there's a lot of knowledge here people should have," Bram said.

"And I read the Basilisk diaries while Reyson was translating them," Felix said. "They are fascinating and I think you're going to love them."

"As soon as George us told fate paired her with you, I started bugging her to bring you here so I could get you these diaries. One of the queens in particular was a fierce warrior who put all the men in their place. She was also brilliant, and she wrote down several potions that got lost in time. There're also things about your venom that I think aren't public knowledge anymore. So, you need to bleed for me because I've been harassing my kid so I could get you these books," Ripley said. "I also have some Basilisk smut if you're into that."

George clearly told her mom about me, but she must have left out a lot because all of her parents were being really nice to me, even if her mom seemed really into the idea of me bleeding into that bowl.

And I didn't feel left out because I wasn't dating George. I loved reading and there wasn't a lot out there about Basilisks. When Ketura and Azren were on this realm, they'd find them and bring them back for me. Sometimes, they were history books and sometimes, they were fiction. It was rarely fiction because the Basilisk was always the villain who met a bad end.

"Basilisk smut?" I asked.

Did I even want to know?

"Oh, yeah. Someone wrote a Basilisk love interest about seven years ago that went viral and it became a thing. Patrons started asking for it, so I started stocking it," Ripley said.

"And Ketura knows you're eighteen now, but she changed your diapers and didn't want to picture you reading that, so she asked me not to buy it, either," Azren said.

"Who reads that?" I demanded.

Ripley and Ravyn started laughing.

"The witches eat it up. They are after a totally different body part now."

I nearly started choking. I grabbed the athame and poked my finger. I needed to bleed in this bowl before someone asked to see my dick.

CHURCH

We all passed the first mom test and got approved for library cards. Which was immensely cool because we all wanted one, but were too terrified of getting declined for a library card to come over and do it. There were places in the library we couldn't go because we weren't approved for them, but there honestly wasn't anything in those areas I would ever need as an energy vampire unless I was up to no good.

I was pretty sure George's mom and aunt broke Drake. George wouldn't have told her mom about how turbulent their relationship was at first, but someone did. They were super accepting, and those diaries were probably going to help him a lot, but I was pretty sure telling him that thirsty witches were more interested in his dick than his toenails just blew his mind.

And then there was Ren, who wasn't letting it drop, and I was pretty sure was winning Ripley over.

"Drake might not be interested in Basilisk smut, but I need to know if your library has something I haven't read yet. I would have told you the witches were probably more interested in your dick than your toenails, but I thought you knew it was a thing and were choosing to ignore it," Ren said.

"I definitely didn't know that was why several witches asked me to join them at the first moon orgy!"

"It was science," Balthazar said, pulling out a pixie stick and dumping it down his throat. "They wanted to know if the Basilisk porn was true."

Felix groaned.

"I thought we hid all the sugar."

"I unhid it," Reyson said. "We're having a celebration. Don't be mean."

"I end up with his glitter all over me every time he finds the sugar!"

Oh, I *adored* George's family. I was used to her dad in history class, but they *all* appeared to be agents of chaos.

"There's *nothing* wrong with glitter," Dexter said.

"Thank you!" Balthazar said.

"If you're a pixie. Balthazar's glitter never washes off. You think it's gone, and then you find it on your balls."

"Disco ball testicles were all the rage back in the day," Loki said.

"Ignore my husband and don't glitter your balls. That's a UTI waiting to happen," Ravyn said.

Dexter was going to Dexter. He winked at Ravyn.

"Unless you're dating a pixie. Then, it just comes with the territory."

George put her hands over her ears and started singing. Dexter did that sometimes because George had a drastic reaction to it. The pixie was the only person bold enough at the table to say something like that in front of parents.

Like, I'd seen the God of Chaos when he was mad at someone. Kaylee and Paris were going to get expelled for attendance at the rate he was going. I was pretty sure he could make true on his threat of making sure their bodies were never found, but he preferred playing with his prey and ruining their lives.

I'm sure he *knew* we were having sex with his little girl, but none of us were about to suggest we were doing anything but chastely holding her hand in case he wanted to get godly about it.

"So, since we're all here and all of you are now family, I need to tell you a secret. Mina, I hope this doesn't change anything," Mags said.

More secrets. George got spooked when she was going to tell us hers. In all fairness, every banshee at the Academy of the Profane shrieking and the God of Death coming to get us because someone got murdered was a pretty big omen, so none of us blamed her. She'd tell us when she was ready, but I was dying to know because I was nosy.

Mags big secret involved Mags, Felix, and Ravyn's husband Killian getting up from the table and taking their clothes off. I didn't know why the witches and warlocks were getting naked, but I knew better than to stare, even though they might be expecting me to look for something.

One, I wouldn't do that to George. Two, Felix and Killian were married and anyone could tell Mags and Matilda were deeply in love. Belladonna would have repeated some outdated nonsense that Matilda was going to fly off and attack us for staring just because she was a shifter, but *no one* liked it if you objectified their partners and everyone reacted badly if it made their partner uncomfortable.

I looked when I heard Mina gasp, but she had permission to look. There had definitely been a witch and two warlocks standing there, but now I was looking at a black cat with white fur on his face, a bat, and George's familiar who was sent away from the academy for pissing on a warlock after he assaulted Matilda.

What.the.fuck?

Mags was a witch. I spent enough time around her with George that there was absolutely no doubt about that. I just met Felix and Killian, but they were definitely warlocks. Everyone knew George's familiar because it was this massive black dog whose breed no one had ever seen before.

We were all just sitting there questioning our life choices that a witch and two warlocks just turned into animals when West fell out laughing.

"Is that a dick on the cat's face?"

I turned my head to the side. I should be losing my shit about all of this, but Felix's cat was all black except for his face. The white fur on his face was definitely in the shape of a dick.

"I gave him that dick shortly before I gave him his body back. Felix, Killian, and Mags started out as familiars. Felix was Ripley's, Killian was Ravyn's, and Lilith hand delivered Mags to George and Matilda's delivery room to be a familiar to both of them. I tried it with Felix because my witch was mad about the dick on his face, but it amused me, so I was never going to remove it. So, I did it again with Killian and later with Mags when the girls were kids."

"So, what are you?" Mina asked.

"I'm a witch who lived a long time ago and died. Lilith

personally asked me if I'd like to stay in the Aether and be reborn with no memories or come back as a familiar and get the chance to mentor twins Lilith wanted looking after. I've always been a lesbian, even when I had to hide it the first time I was alive.

"When Reyson gave me my body back, it was ten-year-old me. I had to go through puberty again right alongside my wards. Matilda and I fell in love and have been together for years. I was just going to be at the academy as a dog, but then Azren took over as headmaster and managed to get me on as a student.

"Then, Matilda and I met you and you're completely perfect. Understand, I didn't want to keep this from you since you've become important to us, but I'm a hybrid now. You're open minded and I know I'm not in any danger from anyone in this room, but other people aren't going to react the same way, so I had to find the *right* time to tell everyone."

We were all holding our breath waiting for Mina to answer. *I* didn't think it was a huge deal. Ren was technically a hybrid, it was just that no one called them that because of all the negative connotations with hybrids. Even West hadn't said anything.

"It doesn't change anything," Mina said. "It's actually badass because you can do totally covert stuff and if you have shifter senses too, you can help stop someone from getting murdered again."

"Wait, do you have shifter senses?" West asked.

"Yeah, I do," Mags said.

"Awesome. Next time the God of Death wants someone to sniff a corpse, that's all you, cupcake. I'm a very sensitive lion."

Loki started laughing.

"Really, Azren? Azren tried to do that to me once, but I'm going to break some of the God of Death's mystique. Azren can shapeshift just as well as I can and is perfectly capable of sniffing their own dead bodies."

"Don't listen to Loki," Azren said. "He's a trickster, and he's just fucking with me. Time was of the essence and if the Paranormal Investigation Bureau was going to solve this, they would have by now. I knew as soon as they found us, they were going to shoo us away, but they even dismissed *me* when I went back alone. But no, West, you can help in different ways."

"How do we stop it from happening again?" Mina demanded.

"I'm working on it. I'm not trying to frighten anyone and this *cannot* leave this room, but a god appears to be using the Academy of the Profane as a killing ground. The board and the Paranormal Investigation Bureau did such a massive coverup that I can't even guess how they are choosing their victims or why it suddenly stops. Church's grandfather said I might be able to piece together *something* from old paper records in a dusty basement, so I'm having boxes brought up from the years I had this same feeling, but as I said, I don't have a ton to go on."

"Why would a god be interested in college students?" Oscar asked. "Like, Kaylee tried to hex George in the back and she and Paris are terrible. Reyson is just trying to get them expelled."

"Most gods *aren't* interested in college students," Reyson said. "Most of them aren't even interested in mortals anymore. They've gone back to their realms so they don't have to deal with them. Even back when there were more of us here, no one was interested in killing them.

Creative punishments are *much* more our style. I couldn't tell you who would do this and why."

"And some of us prefer complicated, flawed mortals over the gods in our family," Loki said.

It was honestly a lot. There was a god brutally murdering people on campus and the other gods didn't know who.

And my girlfriend was keeping an even bigger secret than Mags being a hybrid and her familiar.

GEORGE

I wasn't worried about dinner. I knew my guys and my family were going to get along. I wasn't worried about Dexter or Mina, either. I knew Mags was stressing about telling Mina her secret and she picked a safe space to do it. It was a safe space to reveal mine, too, but I didn't want to step on Mags's big reveal and make it seem like I was trying to overshadow her.

I was bummed Freya wasn't there. She told me what she looked like when she was in her true vessel, but I'd only ever spoken to her as a tiny, gray-haired witch. I could talk to her for hours and it wasn't always curse stuff. She wasn't just a god who had been around for a long time. Freya was different from the other gods I knew.

She'd lived countless *mortal* lifetimes in the bodies of witches. Freya lived for eighteen years with no magic, then had to deal with thinking she was insane when her god memories started to come in. Freya did these *amazing* things as a mortal witch and that resonated with me because of my necklace.

I pulled my Aunt Ravyn aside since Freya was staying at her cottage. She passed the message along that tonight was about everyone meeting our parents and we had a tendency to dominate the conversation when we were together. Freya passed the message along that she absolutely expected me to bring them by for tea so *she* could meet them.

My dad's rotation taking over for Azren was about to be up. Freya had literally been here this entire time to teach all of Azren's classes, but the board wanted Loki next. The *only* reason they seemed to be shitting on Freya was that they didn't know all the contributions she made when she was hiding in witches.

Campus was all aflutter. The dodgeball team Zion put together was good enough to win championships. Oscar should technically be training with a pro team and he showed that on the field. Michael, Drake, and I were signing for him, but the rest of the team had taken up the torch and were learning sign language just in case they were near Oscar and we weren't. Rescinding Oscar's pro offers because he lost his hearing was premature. There were plenty of famous deaf players and it wasn't holding Oscar back *at all.*

Dexter was a short, lean guy, but he was also the fastest person on the team, both on land and in the air. He told me in high school, he played dodgeball and ran track. I'd already talked to Azren about Dexter's request and they said not only was it possible, they had done it before on their realm. They were going to walk me through it, but told me I needed a huge understanding of anatomy and how the muscles would connect, even if I was using cosmic powers. I was hitting the anatomy books every night until I felt ready.

The cheerleaders were another story. I watched practice to support my sister since she always came out for dodgeball practice. Matilda had an amazing group of talented athletes and dancers. Belladonna and Matilda had the *exact* same vision for the squad. Like, I'd never been a cheerleader a single day in my life and even I could tell they were totally sympatico on the direction they wanted to take the cheerleaders. They both wanted to cheer the dodgeball team on, but they wanted the squad to compete, too.

It was like they agreed on everything, but they fought about it, anyway. And it was like, when Belladonna just *let go* and got caught up in something she enjoyed instead of trying so hard to be vampire royalty with shitty beliefs, she just lit up and I could *almost* forget the shitty things she said to my twin just because she was a hellhound.

Belladonna would cut up and get silly with the team then it was like a switch flipped and she remembered she was supposed to think she was better than everyone. I could *see* the thorny stick getting reinserted up her ass, and she usually said something racist to my sister. I'd feel bad for her that she couldn't let herself have fun, but she was taking it out on my sister, so I wasn't a fan.

The next moon orgy was coming up, so if someone wasn't excited about dodgeball or cheerleading, fucking multiple people under the full moon was sure to do it. It wasn't just the fucking. It was the prowling for people to fuck or the anticipation of getting invited if you weren't a witch or a shifter.

"Now that your mom told me about those books, it's even weirder when a witch invites me to join them at the moon orgy. Now I'm not just worried about my hair. They probably have all these weird expectations. Kaylee Krauss invited me and then Paris came right behind her two days later when I told her no. I don't even know what's happening right now," Drake said.

I wasn't dating Drake, so I shouldn't even be worried about who he slept with. But I was butthurt people were asking him. And I was *furious* Kaylee and Paris did. And I knew I had no right to be, so I just savagely bit into my bread and sulked.

"It's not just the books," West said. "I'm telling you this as a very secure straight man. You're a sexy ginger, a college dodgeball player, everyone *loves* the goalie, and you're a musician and composer. Everyone in Sigmis dorm has walked by your dorm and heard you playing. Fucking you has that added level of danger because your entire body is venomous. You're walking sex. *Of course,* you're going to get invited to the moon orgy."

"Dude," Ren said. "You can't say shit like that and go around kissing men and insist you're totally straight."

"One, I never slipped anyone the tongue. You can totally kiss your friends if there's no tongue. Two, would you prefer I be one of those toxic bros who insults you and starts fights rather than compliment you when you *clearly* need it?"

"He has a point," Church said. "And he hasn't kissed me yet."

"'Yet,'" Oscar said.

"Do you need a pick-me-up lion kiss, Church?" West asked.

"No! But I'll take a George kiss."

"This is big," West said. "This is the last moon orgy before Yule break. We have to make it big for everyone because we're going to be apart."

West, Oscar, and Ren were going back home to California. Church lived in Profane. Azren was bringing Drake home to visit with Ketura and take care of business back on their realm. Mina was from New Orleans and she was going home. Dexter had a bit of a tumultuous relationship with his parents because they wanted him to pay for his transition himself and they didn't know his grandfather was paying for his T. Dexter was going to be staying with us.

"I'm okay with not doing the moon orgy," Drake said.

"You can come play with us!" a thirsty witch at the next table giggled.

I stared her down, even though I had no right to. Drake wasn't my boyfriend, and I was still processing the fact that I was even mad about it. And then I realized Drake was staring at *me*. Shit. I wasn't trying to get caught because I didn't even know what I was feeling yet.

"Can I talk to you in my dorm for a second?"

Fuuuuck.

I followed Drake to his dorm, and the door was open. I didn't think much about it since he had a roommate, but when we walked in, Kaylee came out of his bathroom. Drake immediately changed. His eyes changed to slits and his fangs came down. He was probably calling his venom. Shit. I was immune to him, but he looked scary.

"What *the fuck* are you doing in my dorm room?"

Kaylee just giggled like an idiot.

"Relax. Your roommate let me in. I thought I'd give you another chance to reconsider joining me at the moon orgy."

"Try again. My roommate knows I can't stand you," Drake growled.

"Because you don't know me. You should definitely go to the moon orgy with me."

"Get the fuck out of my dorm room. I'm going with George."

What? I mean, I wasn't mad at the idea. I was kind of into it, really. Kaylee stomped her foot like a child and went storming out of the room.

"This is *all your fault,* George!" she shrieked.

Yeah, it was always my fault when it came to Kaylee Krauss. She slammed the door and Drake turned to me.

"Sorry, I just blurted that out, but I meant it. And you seemed mad at the idea of me going with someone else."

"Because I was! And it didn't make sense because a few weeks ago, we couldn't stand each other. But everything West said is true. You're insanely hot, goalies are sexy, you're like walking sex when you play the violin, *and* you compose, and I completely love that you give me a hard time and don't treat me like the sun shines out of my ass."

That part was vital, and I didn't want it to change when they all found out I was a god. Loki and my dad were a little more humble because they fell in love and handfasted into covens with people who revered them as gods, but absolutely called them out when they were being ridiculous. People were going to change when I took my necklace off and I didn't want any of my guys to. I liked my relationship with Drake. If we were going to take it to the next step, I was into that, but I didn't want Drake's whole personality to change.

Drake stepped forward and yanked me to his chest.

"*Never* tell anyone I said this because I have a reputation, but the sun *does* shine out of your ass and the music has been flowing since we decided we didn't hate each other. I'm always going to be the kind of man that is going to support the shit out of everything you do but with my own brand of snark."

"And I'm always going to be the woman who wants and needs that. Promise no matter what happens, that doesn't change."

"I'd pinky swear, but I'm about to kiss you."

"You'd better make it good because—"

"Shut up, George."

And then Drake took my breath away kissing me. It was the kind of kiss you gave someone when you spent weeks loathing them, decided to tolerate them because the fates said they were the only way you'd get answers, then you realized they were kind of amazing, and you got irrationally angry at the idea of anyone else inviting them to the moon orgy.

It was *that* kind of scorching kiss.

My knees felt like jelly and I wanted more. Drake stopped me when I started tugging at his shirt. West was spot on about something else, too. Even though I was immune, the fact that Drake's entire body was venomous was exciting.

"Oh, no, George. You aren't getting all this until the full moon."

I poked him in the chest.

"You're lucky you're a goalie *and* play the violin because that's mean as hell."

That asshole kissed me the exact same way again and *kicked me out of his dorm.*

"Anticipation makes it feel better when it finally happens, George!" he called to my back.

I didn't turn around and threw up double middle fingers at him. Bell women didn't beg for sex.

AZREN

There were probably a ton of people on this realm who would kill to be the headmaster of The Academy of the Profane. Some of these assholes who ran this place probably did. There was currently an overlooked warlock teaching Dark Arts who not only *wanted* the job but would be better at it than me and the person I was filling in for.

I was fucking miserable.

My happy place was teaching. Not only was I kicked out of my classroom, but I had the whole board up my ass all the time and I kept having to cancel my private lessons with George. She had become the high point of my day and so I was spoiling the shit out of her when I had her alone. She'd never been treated like a god by someone who wasn't her family because of that necklace and she needed it.

If I wasn't dealing with the board demanding I clean up the mess they thought I'd made giving Fleur's coven closure and letting the student body know to watch their backs so they didn't end up next, I had to deal with shrieking freshmen. Two in particular.

The *only* reason Reyson agreed to come lecture for a few weeks was because someone finally asked when his kids were here. Loki had never been asked, and he was up next. Freya loved teaching just as much as I did. She taught Odin himself, but the board was greedy and wanted as many gods as I could bring.

Reyson hadn't disappeared a student and by all reports, nearly everyone was having a blast in his class. The two that weren't had been camping out in my new office bothering me about it. Yeah, I *could* have told Reyson to stop kicking Kaylee out for tardiness and insulting Paris for defending her, but I wasn't.

The two of them needed to learn that life wasn't fair and actions had consequences. It didn't matter how powerful your name or family was, there was always going to be someone who outranked you. The board was going to give Kaylee two more strikes. If someone didn't catch those on video like Dexter had, Lindsay wasn't going to enforce it and expel her when she did.

Reyson was just helping the process along.

"When is he leaving?" Kaylee shrieked.

She shrieked a lot. It was like nails down a chalkboard. If she wasn't yelling, she was stomping her foot like a child. She was way too old to be doing that. Lindsay had a *bad* case of pustules. She was probably going to be out longer than the usual two months.

"His last day is right before Yule break," I sighed.

"He should have been gone before that!" Paris said.

"I hate to break it to you, but Loki is up next. If you think you're getting fucked with now, you haven't seen anything yet, cupcake. Loki is George Bell's uncle, and he also saw that video. Maybe you shouldn't throw hexes when people's backs are turned. How's your mom, by the way?"

The problem here was that these two women thought I was the more reasonable god, and I definitely wasn't. I was less antagonistic than Reyson and Loki, but there was always a point when I became an utter asshole and we were pretty much there.

"My mom is going to *fire* your ass when she gets back."

"Yeah, you're letting a teacher abuse us!"

"If you can't handle someone being mean to you, you're never going to make it in the real world. And I'm not going anywhere. You might. Your mom might, too. I've been cleaning up her messes since you hexed her. Now, unless you have a *legitimate* complaint and not just people treating you exactly the way the two of you and your mother have treated the other students, get the fuck out of my office. And don't come back unless you're dying and need my help.

"Because I'm *not* the nice god here. I'm Death incarnate and you do not want to piss me off any further than you already have. You little girls think because I've tolerated you so far and have been polite that I'm not dangerous. The other *gods* are afraid of me so show some fucking respect. I've got gods in time out in my realm and I've reaped kings and queens. I helped create the universe. Your drama is nothing to me and I could easily unmake the both of you because you're annoying."

I may have amplified my voice, called my scythe, and let my black smoke fill the room. Kaylee and Paris fled in terror. I hadn't done that in a long time. At some point in my long existence, I just decided I was too old to be terrifying mortals with parlor tricks.

But that felt good. Kaylee was a menace and Paris was

egging her on. I was furious Kaylee flung a hex at George's back, too. It wouldn't have done anything to George, but she would have had to explain *why* it didn't. Witches could shield, but it would have been weird for her to have one up walking the hallway with her twin sister when she thought she was alone.

And new witches had terrible aim unless they played sports in high school. Kaylee and Paris weren't even trying to support the new dodgeball and cheerleading teams. Zion Skinner wanted both of them removed from magical combat because not only was their aim shitty in class, they weren't even *trying* to improve it.

They hit several people they weren't sparring with in magical combat, but the board wasn't considering the bigger implication there with Kaylee's next two strikes. That hex hit Lindsay because Dexter yelled to duck and George made sure Matilda went down with her. It could have easily hit Matilda or Dexter. According to Zion, the only reason it didn't was because the twins ducked and Dexter saw her getting ready to throw it.

My hands were tied by the board. All I could do was lecture her and it went in one ear and out the next. Kaylee knew she had two strikes. All she had to do was wait it out until Lindsay was back to make them and she could have as many strikes as she wanted.

And I knew damned well Lindsay didn't tell Kaylee to stop digging on the internet for awful curses and focus on her schoolwork. No, they both blamed George for this, like George forced Kaylee to look up diabolical hexes and fling one at her back. The one person Kaylee would actually listen to was just as immature as she was.

Supernaturals tended to come in three categories. They prayed to the god who created them and left offerings.

Some thought the gods were just a metaphor because honestly, we didn't get involved with them much anymore. Loki and Reyson were the most out and proud gods on this realm. They had a channel where they did videos together. I was on their show once.

The third kind of supernatural was the one who had either seen their show or met them and *knew* the gods were real, but something terrible happened in their life and the god that created them didn't swoop in and make it better, so they were angry at them. They didn't leave offerings or pray, and they shit talked in private, but if they came face to face with the god who created them, they'd respectfully demand to know why their prayers weren't answered.

Then, you had Kaylee and Lindsay Krauss. Kaylee was in preschool with George and Matilda. They thought George was a witch, but Reyson was highly involved in all his kid's lives. They saw a god being a good dad and thought that meant we were all harmless.

Lilith made sure they lost their lawsuit against a kid, but George never really told Lilith or Reyson how bad Kaylee was. George always treated her more like a nuisance than a menace, which I *guess* I got in middle school.

I'd never reveal George's secret before she was ready, but Kaylee was going to keep hurting people who weren't invincible trying to take her out.

So, I was going to have a blast showing Kaylee and Lindsay Krauss why people feared the gods. I'd totally play the villain for George.

GEORGE

The whole campus was excited about the moon orgy. Ren gifted me matching earrings he stole when he brought me my latte with breakfast. Ren brought me random stolen things all the time, but they only matched when he was really trying to make an impression. When he was trying to tell me he was impressed with my dodgeball skills, he stole someone's shoes.

They were those expensive designer shoes that a lot of people collected and they definitely belonged to a bear shifter with gigantic feet because as soon as he realized they were missing, he started interrogating people. I didn't have giant bear shifter feet. Those shoes were never going to fit me and even if they did, I couldn't wear them on campus without getting body tackled by an angry bear who was going to rip them off my feet because my boyfriend's Kitsune really liked to steal for people he cared about.

Drake was still kissing me like *that*. He was a damned vag tease because right when I got into it and was about to throw him down and get filthy in front of the entire student body, he just stopped, smacked me on the ass, and then quoted Dr. Frankenfurter.

Apparently, *Rocky Horror* had made its way to Azren's realm like it had Hell. It was a big hit in the supernatural world. A demon got obsessed and brought it to Hell. Azren was the one who brought it home to the Netherworld. At the rate Drake was giving me the anticipation line, I was wondering how many realms out there I hadn't been to yet had the urge yell *Janet* anytime someone said Damn it.

And Drake was an asshole for making me wonder about that. I was totally crazy about him.

The only thing I was missing was Azren and they definitely couldn't be there without getting fired. My alone time with Azren kept getting interrupted by the board. I wouldn't even be mad about it if they were discussing protocols to keep the students safe. Everyone but Church's grandfather wanted Azren to lie and say they were mistaken about a student getting murdered.

They wanted Azren to say they overreacted and Fleur just disappeared. Which was fucking stupid because Azren was the God of Death and no one was going to believe them that they got something like that wrong.

I missed my Azren time. Not only were they helping me figure out my magic and teaching me all kinds of different perspectives, but Azren took pampering to the next level. They could even distract me from how much I wanted more, they were that good at making a woman feel cherished.

I was *going* to get Azren naked soon.

It was finally time for the moon orgy. The dining hall didn't serve a full dinner when there was a moon orgy. People usually brought picnic baskets out to Halliwell Square and could pick up sandwiches, finger foods, and desserts. Some people were dumb enough to try to have food delivered right before it started like all the supernatural restaurants and delivery companies weren't closed because of the moon orgy and this place was warded against humans, so their delivery drivers would never find the Academy of the Profane.

West bought a mini fridge for their dorm and picked up sandwiches from a deli I loved. They also had amazing cookies baked with magic. They met me at my dorm with a picnic basket and blankets.

Matilda was already out in Halliwell Square with Mags and Mina. Now that she was co-captain of the cheerleading squad, everyone knew who she was. There were a ton of people coming to our table in the dining hall about joining her. My sister was a *massive* flirt. She was always much better at that than I was, but she was picky about the people she kept close to her. She might be interested in bringing someone else into her pack, but right now, she only had eyes for Mags and Mina.

Halliwell Square was decked out with witch and pixie lights again. There was another band playing, but it wasn't the same group of sirens as before. No, that band was currently on blankets and pillows having a *very* good time with a pack of shifters.

The current band was fantastic. It was West that nodded to the band this time. I expected some song I said I loved on social media ages ago because West probably stalked me, too. I *was not* expecting what the band started playing. Everyone paused their fucking for a minute to shoot a what the fuck look at the band. I fell out laughing because it was just *so* West.

"What did you promise the sirens to get them to Rick Roll the entire moon orgy?"

"Nothing. They thought it was ridiculous, and inappropriate, and they were jealous they didn't think of it first. This was just to make you smile, but there's probably someone here who just got invited to their first moon orgy and needed a laugh."

"Me. It's my first moon orgy," Drake said. "I'm not nervous, though."

I was, and this wasn't even my first one. It was my first time with Drake. I knew the theory behind creating a new magical race, but that didn't automatically make me good at sex. West, Church, Oscar, and Ren liked it, but Drake was an entirely new person I hadn't had sex with yet. What if I went to kiss him and accidentally broke his nose?

"That's some bullshit, Baby Drake," West said. "I'd been to loads of moon orgies and have had cougars after my nuts since I was illegal, but none of them were George. I made a playbook and Church was rude as hell and wouldn't even look at it."

"I peeked," Ren said. "You should have asked Oscar to draw it because what you had those stick figures doing isn't possible with a skeleton."

"You lie!" West gasped. "My playbook was *genius.*"

"I'm pretty sure one of the stick figures that was supposed to be George was missing a head."

West tossed his mane over his shoulder, then set to putting it up in a messy bun.

"Well, *I'm* the only person here who has fucked five people at the same time under the full moon, so you're going to want my expertise so none of you end up breaking your dick. Because that happened to a really enthusiastic Unseelie once and it ruined the whole moon orgy. I'm the official moon orgy coach. Let me guide you into the group fucking. Everyone sit down and eat because we're going to need calories and carbs to fuck all night. Shit. I should have had Ren steal Zion's whistle so I could be all official."

"Oh, hell no," Ren said. "I'm going to let you have the moon orgy coach thing because I don't want a broken dick, but I only steal from people who annoy me."

I dug into my sandwich. I loved watching them just talk, and that they got along so well.

"Why'd you steal that bear shifter's expensive shoes?" I asked.

"There's another freshman Kitsune in my classes and he's completely gross about the fact that she's Japanese American. He keeps fetishizing her because she's Asian. That's the *only* thing he likes about her because he hasn't tried to get to know her. He keeps cornering her and saying gross things instead of *trying* to get to know her.

"She wants to handle it and thinks she can do it in a way that she earns her second tail. We have a bet going on who has the most when we graduate and I'm ahead. Minako can get her own revenge and I'm not going to take that from her, but I had this deep-seated need to steal that fucker's shoes."

"They would have fit me better than they fit George," Oscar pointed out.

Ren fell out laughing.

"Yeah, but George wasn't going to *wear* them and get assaulted by that fucker. You would have beat his ass, baby, and I promised Minako no one was going to do that but her."

"Love you, sweetie," Oscar said, blowing Ren a kiss.

Those two together were adorable. They were supportive of each other and just fit together just right. And they were letting me be a part of it. I was just watching them and smiling like a total idiot. I realized Drake was, too. My Basilisk was secretly a romantic, even if he pretended like he wasn't and kissed me like *that*.

"Okay, as your official moon-orgy coach, put your trash away and limber up. Get those *muscles* good and stretched because in addition to no broken dicks, I'm dating a good bit of the dodgeball team, so there will be no pulled muscles that sideline our best players. I *wish* I had that whistle so I could motivate you when we run laps."

"We're *not* running laps," Church said. "I've got vampire speed, but I don't enjoy running. If I run, it's because a bigger predator than a vampire is chasing me. And I'm not scared of lions if your lizard brain was thinking about shifting and chasing me to get me to run."

"Chasing a naked vampire could be kinky," West said.

"You're definitely not totally straight," Oscar said.

"Kinky for *George*. She's the only one I'm interested in seeing naked. I'm ignoring all the extra dicks and what you're going to be doing with them that don't involve pleasing my girlfriend because *she's* into it."

Drake raised his hand.

"I'd like to get on with pleasing George instead of talking about running laps and your straightness."

"Yes, straight to business," West said. "Drake and George are going to work out all that sexual tension because George might actually maul him if he kisses her and stops again. We've been watching you, girl. You want that Basilisk dick *bad*. Church and I are going to watch Drake and George, and Ren and Oscar are going to show George how they like it with each other. I wrote a playbook for this, too, and some of you are going to have a 'come to

Bastet' talk with yourself about how *good* my orgy play-books are."

I grabbed Drake and kissed him.

"I like West's plan. We're doing that."

"Oh, thank you because waiting was miserable, but I wanted it to be special," Drake said, doing that thing with the kissing again.

It was *finally* happening with Drake and me.

GEORGE

The anticipation was there the first time I had sex with all these men. I was nervous and waiting for it. It was different with Drake. Drake *kicked me out of his dorm* and made me wait for it. And then he kept doing the kissy and booty-spanking thing and *still* telling me no.

It was infuriating and hot as fuck because I rarely got told no unless I was being completely unreasonable. And when I took my necklace off, most people were going to try to make it happen even if I *was* being unreasonable about it. West did that before he even figured out my secret. I wasn't mad about it because that was just West.

Drake wasn't going to treat me any differently when he found out because he grew up around Azren, I didn't think Church, Ren, or Oscar would, either. For now, I was going to enjoy Drake.

And I was. Drake had a god in his life who was respectful of women. Azren had shapeshifted into a woman and lived that way for a while before they settled on nonbinary. I hadn't had sex with Azren yet, but they definitely knew how to spoil a woman.

Drake was very respectfully manhandling me just right. He had me on my back with my arms pinned over my head and Drake knew all the right places to lick and bite. He never bit hard enough to break the skin because even without his fangs and purposely calling his venom, he could kill someone if he did. He bit just enough to make you think he might. Drake could only break my skin if I let him and I was immune to his venom, but fuck me if my heart didn't race every time he bit down.

"West, get over here and hold her down," Drake ordered.

Bossy pants. Drake was *bossy*. West was the kind of lion who didn't deal well with authority figures and orders. He was the kind of boyfriend you had to ask a certain way or he'd do the exact opposite. Unless you were Drake and the request was kinky.

Drake didn't even say *please* and West was already up. He hauled my head into his lap and wrapped my arms around his waist.

"Pretend you can't kick my ass when you aren't holding back and don't let go," West whispered.

"Oh, I'm right where I want to be," I said, stealing a kiss.

West guided me to look at Drake. Drake was hovering over me with snake eyes and a forked tongue. A few iridescent blue and green scales had broken out along his forehead and temples. He'd gone snake, but his fangs weren't out. I drew in a breath. I wanted to touch him, but I was pretty sure that was against the rules.

"You're beautiful like this. And you're mine. If any witch tries to come for what's mine, they are going to find out the hard way that I've been holding back with Kaylee."

"Personally, I think you should go full out, give her a zap that her ancestors feel in the Aether, and make all the body hair she wants disappear, but all the body hair she waxes grow uncontrollably," Ren said. "Stealing from her doesn't even make me feel better."

I groaned.

"I'm in my happy place right now. Please do not mention my nemesis."

"I don't want to talk about her, either," Drake said, biting my nipples. "The vibe in my dorm room was terrible after she broke in. It took four days to cleanse her aura out. I've been waiting for this."

"Bitch, you were the one who wanted to wait! You kissed me like that, smacked my ass, quoted *Rocky Horror*, and kicked me out of your dorm room."

"Bitch, I had to plan. I didn't draw stick figures fucking or write a playbook, but I had to plan. Now, shut your mouth," Drake said, biting me.

Bossy.

I went with it because I was finally getting what I wanted. Forked tongues were officially one of my new favorite things. Drake was flicking it all over my body and leaving little bites on the way down. I spread my legs because that was where this was headed and he *spanked* me again.

"So greedy," he hissed.

"I'm not holding her down and I'm kicking you out of the orgy if you don't eat pussy, man," West said.

"I'm *so* eating this pussy, but I haven't paid any attention to these thighs. George has *fabulous* legs."

"I'll allow it. Proceed," Church said.

Drake licked and nipped my thighs until I was about to go crazy. He'd get right near my clit and back off. I was writing and kept thrusting my hips at him to give him a hint. Bell women didn't beg, but we would shove our pussies in your face to give you a hint. Asshole. My latest boyfriend was an asshole, and I was crazy about him.

I stole some of my mom's Basilisk smut and they *never* mentioned the forked tongue, which led me to believe these writers didn't do proper research because when Drake finally went for it, my eyes went back in my head.

Drake had *skills, and* I forgot how much I wanted to beat his ass for kissing me like that and then kicking me out of his dorm room. And, oh fuck. He had those dexterous fingers that flew over a violin and made such beautiful music. Drake definitely knew how to play a woman with them.

Oscar was on his knees showing me how Ren liked his dick sucked. I knew how Oscar liked it. I hadn't forgotten how Oscar fucked my mouth. Ren wasn't as aggressive as Oscar. He was a little cheekier about it and his tails were flicking every time Oscar did something he liked. I also adore the little fox noises he made.

I couldn't even deal with life right now. I didn't last long at all before Drake played my body right into an intense orgasm. And I couldn't even move because Drake had my lower half pinned down and West was holding my top half. I could have thrown them both off if I wanted to, but I didn't. I liked feeling like I couldn't move.

Drake had planned what he wanted to do, so I was following along. He spent all this time worshipping my body and pleasing me and I definitely wasn't a selfish lover.

"Can I return the favor?"

"Another night. I'm still going to give you a hard time because you *like* it, but consider tonight me showing you how much I appreciate you sticking it out when I was being cruel because I thought all witches were the same. I was wrong. Mags and the rest of your family are amazing, too. Your mom and aunt are fantastic. Consider orgasms under the full moon my apology."

"I accepted that ages ago, but I'll accept orgasms as apologies the next time any of you piss me off. I'm a *big* fan of that tongue and those fingers, but are you going to show me what that big dick can do?"

"If you don't, *I'm* kicking you out of the moon orgy," Oscar said. "I knew this was headed here the second day we ate together, and she told you to get fucked when you insulted her again."

I didn't.

Drake slithered on top of me and kissed me. He guided himself inside me.

"Wrap your legs around my waist and don't let go of West."

"Yes, sir," I said, happily snagging his hips with my legs.

I didn't realize how expressive snake eyes were. Drake *liked* that I called him sir, and he enjoyed that I was doing exactly what he asked. I loved it, too. Drake stilled and looked down at me.

"If you told me a year ago I'd be at a moon orgy with a witch and feeling like this about her, I probably would have started a fight."

"Show me."

This probably didn't make any fucking sense to anyone who hadn't done it before, but Drake made love like a virtuoso violinist. He took control of my body and played it like a master. It was intense and just as passionate as the music Drake composed.

He took his time building up the pleasure and I just let him play my body. West had me completely pinned down, and that just added to the sensation. I was so fucking close.

"West, pinch her nipples," Drake hissed.

And I was done. West knew how I liked my nipples handled and he did it just right. I completely came undone. Drake must have asked West for an assist because he was waiting for me. A snake rattle came out of Drake when he came and it was just so fucking hot.

As the aftershocks were still hitting me, Drake rested his forehead on mine.

"Now, wrap your arms around me and hold me for a bit."

I'd hold my demanding Basilisk whenever he asked for it, even if it wasn't really an ask.

DRAKE

George was perfect and so unexpected. I didn't just put her off until the moon orgy because I wanted it to be perfect. That was a big part of it, too. It was a Basilisk thing. Nothing seemed to scare her but yet was the operative word here.

I was like Ren, even if we were created by different gods. Basilisks could half shift like Kitsunes could, but most people didn't find us cute. And I took George's mom up on her offer and borrowed one of those Basilisk smut books because I was curious. They didn't even mention it. It was mostly about us being venomous.

Snakes were docile *unless* you threatened their territory. Snaking out when my emotions were high was still something I was working on. Azren had been teaching me meditation for years for when I turned eighteen. I could usually stop it before it spread past my eyes.

But I was nervous, terrified, and worried about pleasing

her. I couldn't focus on my breathing and keeping the snake at bay. At most, I could keep my fangs and venom from coming out. But she wasn't scared. I was sure she read those books her mom suggested to me because she read a lot. She wouldn't have expected it.

George wasn't lying when she told me I was beautiful like that. She really did like it and that made me feel good because this was a part of me. She had no desire to hurt me or use anything about me. George was the strongest person in this academy and I thought she liked and appreciated me taking control.

It was interesting being watched by my new friends. It was actually a turn on. Now, it was my turn to watch. I participated as we all kissed and touched her to get her ready again, but I was going to need a little more time before my dick could go again. We all caressed and kissed her until she said she was ready.

West was a lot, but I really liked him. I still couldn't believe he kissed me when he found out I was a goalie. I was raised by a pansexual reaper who usually preferred women and a pansexual, shapeshifting, nonbinary god who had never been in a relationship the entire time I'd known them. I preferred men, and I was pretty sure Church did, too. West kissed a *lot* of men for a dude who talked about how straight he was.

I didn't draw a stick-figure orgy playbook, but I did plan exactly what I was going to do to her. Fuck it. Watching West's plan come to life, I was definitely drawing stick figures next time. At first, I thought he was crazy, but it was coming together nicely, even if Ren didn't steal Zion's whistle. Ren stole me one sock once. It was a little weird.

West flopped on his back after they all spent this time prepping George.

"Get over here and slide that ass down my dick."

We all groaned as George made a big show of lining West's cock up against her ass and slowly working it into her. She sighed when she had all of him. I loved her little sex noises. George leaned back against West and he wrapped his arms around her waist to support her.

"Ren and Oscar, pick a top and a bottom," West said.

"I want George this time and I want you to pull my tails," Ren said.

Oscar's eyes darkened.

"Done."

Damn. This had the potential to be insanely hot. Ren slid into George. While I was making love to George, Ren and Oscar were giving us a show, so they were ready. She was watching them when I was going down on her, but she was totally focused on me after. Oscar squeezed the lube on Ren's ass and started working himself in Ren's ass.

Fuck that was hot. But West wasn't done. I couldn't go again yet. My cock was hard from the show, but I'd be useless. Church was another story and West made damned sure he wasn't left out.

And how magnificent was George? She had a lion in her ass, a Kitsune in her pussy, an energy vampire in her mouth, and she was being fucked by extension by a brujo. George wasn't faking it. No one was. She was having the time of her life and she was powerful like this.

We were all powerful supernaturals, and we were here to please her. Love potions were against the law. They didn't make anyone fall in love. They got dangerously obsessed and usually ended up killing the person who gave them the potion. Back in the day, that was punishment enough, but people evolved and eventually changed their thinking that trying to manipulate people's minds and feelings wasn't right.

Not even a god could force someone to fall in love with them. They had to earn it just like everyone else. And she earned it. Two of us wanted nothing to do with her because of the Kaylee drama. I hated her just because she was a witch.

George won us all over. She even changed my opinion about all witches. Watching her take on four men at once was glorious, especially *these* four men. George had a filthy mouth, and she was totally egging them on every time she took Church's dick out of her mouth.

I grabbed my cock and started slowly stroking it. Not hard. There was something about the full moon that made everyone go longer and refractory periods were shorter. I was definitely feeling it. I was so going to have her again if she wanted to keep going.

The tableau in front of me was getting frenzied. Church had taken over and was fucking her face. Ren got feral every time Oscar yanked on one of his tails. Oscar probably knew more about what Ren liked than any of us and I was learning. West was pumping her ass and kept biting her shoulder.

I'd only been with her once, but she liked getting bit.

Church finished first and collapsed on the blanket. Ren was about to lose his mind from all the attention to his tails. He shoved his hand between him and George and started working her clit with his thumb. West shifted his grip to pinch her nipples.

George came hard. When I was inside her, she clamped down on my cock and milked me. I *knew* what it felt like when she came. It wasn't super shocking that when I heard that beautiful noise she made when an orgasm hit, West and Ren weren't that far behind, which just set off Oscar.

George had this beautiful, post orgasmic blush on her breasts, but before we could snuggle and enjoy the afterglow, the one thing no one wanted to hear filled the Academy of the Profane.

The Banshees were screaming again.

AZREN

I hoped I'd at least have *something* before another student died. I had hoped making it public knowledge that a student had been murdered would make them wary of strangers, even if they happened to be gods. They'd heard enough lectures between Reyson and me that we were powerful and petty, but not omnipotent.

I knew it was *a* god, but I couldn't figure out which one or why they were doing this. We could do a lot of things, but we couldn't override free will. We were also the Queens of gaslighting and manipulation with words, but actually messing with people's minds using divine magic tended to melt their brains.

Narrowing the gods down to someone who might have been given that power was difficult. We weren't all friends. Some pantheons were vast with gods of totally minor things. Some of them had a lot of sex with each other and produced a ton of children. Some of those families were toxic as fuck, but were more about petty curses.

So, yeah, I was lost. I didn't know who decided to violently murder a witch or who could cover their tracks like that.

And it happened again under my watch. I needed another god's eyes on this, but I couldn't go to my old friends. Loki and Freya didn't really get involved with the other families. Reyson destroyed their societies, but he found a lot of the other gods insufferable. He wouldn't know, either. No, I needed George because she was a student and might know something about the victim.

Problem was, there was a moon orgy going on and Drake was with her this time. I was happy for them. George was good for Drake. I was crazy about George, but if Drake wasn't okay with it, I'd step back.

I was throwing my clothes on rather than magick them on because I was putting off crashing the moon orgy. I'd actually been napping. There was a knock on my door. It was everyone. Even Mags, Matilda, and Mina were there.

"Dodgeball field again?" Matilda asked.

"Shrieking Woods."

"Oh, fuck no," Matilda said. "That's where all the deranged ghosts hang out. How do we know the Banshee in Shrieking Woods didn't get someone who got drunk and wandered away from the moon orgy? The junior shifters have been brewing moonshine in some of the empty faculty cabins. It was pretty potent. At least one pixie got super drunk and started a brawl with some older vampires. I get that you can disrespect ghosts and not get dick punched like Church, but can you control an entire fucking *forest* of serial-killer ghosts?"

"Exactly," West said. "I don't know what's worse—getting murdered or getting punched in the dick."

This conversation would be so much funnier if there

wasn't a dead body in Shrieking Woods. I laughed when I heard about the ruse because it was very much my old friend. It was *still* amusing now that I was on campus and hearing how the legends grew since this campus was founded.

"Truth time and this cannot leave this cabin. Shrieking Woods isn't more or less haunted than the rest of these grounds. The rest of the ghosts didn't banish all the bad ghosts there, and the Banshee is an urban legend. There are a ton of rare and delicate plants that grow in Shrieking Woods that don't need to be trampled on by students. A lot of them are used in healing potions, but many college students are going to rip them up, roll them in a joint, and smoke them because they can also get you high.

"There's a cabin with a caretaker who deals with the rare plants. If it's a student and not the caretaker, they might have seen something and hid. The cabin is hard to find unless you know where to look. Of course, the person doing this might have already figured that out and done this when they were traveling for work. Though, most of you don't work when the moon is full."

The caretaker was *always* some type of Fae or green witch. Someone with a deep connection to nature, but could also handle it if someone was in the forest who wasn't supposed to be. They also had to be level-headed enough to *scare* college students and not maim them. None of them were dumb enough to take on a god. They would have called for backup.

No one called me, so they were either dead, completely out of the forest for the night, or for some reason called the Paranormal Investigation Bureau when a god crashed their woods instead of another god. The caretaker could have been invited to their own moon orgy since that's what most of the faculty was doing tonight.

I didn't know what I was going to find when I brought all these college students straight to a dead body in a forest Beatrix Halliwell built up such an urban legend about hundreds of years ago, students were still scared to go in.

Another witch with her heart surgically cut out. Fleur wasn't in my history class, so I didn't know much about her. This one, I knew. Saffron Dukes was a brilliant history student who challenged me in class with these amazing questions. She was a junior who told me after class once that she was doing independent study in potions. She'd already come up with a brand new healing potion for the common cold when she was a sophomore.

"Damn," Mina said. "Saffron was just as well loved as Fleur was. Some of her healing potions were more effective than what they give you at the infirmary or you can buy at the supernatural market. She never charged the students for them because she said it was a learning experience. Some of the legacy students tried to pressure her into making them unaffordable so she'd have a cushion when she graduated. Saffron was a scholarship student. She could have used the money, but then the rest of the scholarship students couldn't afford it."

Two victims. Two beloved witches who were so insanely talented in their chosen fields, they were doing things most people their age couldn't do. I had a pretty good idea *how* they were choosing their victims, but not why.

"Does it smell like the same person did this?" I asked.

West shot me a withering look.

"You know damned well it's the damn person without asking me to sniff a murder victim."

West complained, but West, Mags, and Matilda did the shifter thing. The MO was the same, but a second strong witch as a victim had just put another theory in my head. The shifters agreed it was the same killer, but the second theory was still pretty strong.

Before I could even voice it or call Saffron from the void to find out if she knew anything, I had the same pissed-off detectives from the Paranormal Investigation Bureau as the first time this happened kicking *me* off a murder scene like this wasn't my domain.

I portalled them all back to my cabin and conjured some food. They probably ate before the moon orgy, then built up a sweat and might be hungry again. I ate my feelings when I was thinking, so I needed the food.

I needed details about Saffron that I wouldn't be privy to as her teacher, but they would as her classmates. The Paranormal Investigation Bureau was going to summon her and traumatize her spirit. I'd be able to swoop in to take her to the Aether when they did the rites, but I didn't trust the Paranormal Investigation Bureau to be delicate with her before she got to me.

The caretaker never came out, so I was guessing they were at a moon-orgy celebration. If there were cameras out here, one of George's dads could hack anything with a Wi-Fi connection and could get me the footage.

But first, food and questioning the living.

GEORGE

I was nowhere near as smart as Azren and I could only use their power when they were close to me. They'd been teaching me, but their board kept stealing Azren, and my private lessons kept getting canceled. I was just a stupid eighteen-year-old, even if I happened to be a god.

Even I could see the similarities between the victims. I think we all did. No one had to say it. None of us were idiots. Someone was murdering insanely-gifted witches. The question was, why?

"Did Saffron have a coven?" Azren asked. "She stayed to talk to me after class because she was fascinated with history and the gods, but we never talked about her love life."

Mina just rolled her eyes.

"You've clearly never been to college. The legacy students are all here fishing for mates. If you're a scholarship student who wants to focus on your education and happen to be talented, you've got people throwing themselves at you. Do you know how many boys at this school thought I'd just get over the fact that I'm not into dick at all because I happen to be powerful? *Of course,* she has a coven. Saffron has had men and women throwing themselves at her since it became apparent she was that gifted in potions."

"I'll need names. I can't question Saffron now, but I'll probably get more information about her behavior from her coven."

"Why would a god target powerful witches?" Ren asked.

"It could be a god, but I'm also thinking it might be an angel. The god that created them broke a lot of rules the gods agreed to follow when they first started making living beings. They've also historically taken issues with Lilith and her creations.

"I've had their god in a jar in time out in my realm for a very long time because of it. I had hoped it would give his angels some kind of life where they could love who they wanted and figure out what kind of life they wanted when they were allowed to have free will without getting punished. They've stopped ambushing my reapers to demand their god back for a while now, but there could be one psycho who is still following orders."

It was a theory. Lucifer and Samael told us about their brothers and Lilith told us stories about how she had to create Hell because the angels were being terrible. Lilith took demons and Hellhounds to her realm and created witches who were more capable of fighting back and left them on this one.

"Wouldn't a rogue angel be more interested in my brother? He was born to a witch and a warlock who descended from Lucifer. If this angel was carrying old grudges, I think he'd be more interested in the brother who turned his back on his family and god than random witches at the Academy of the Profane. Plus, angels aren't meant to love anyone but the god who created them. I think one of them would be after my brother because he's in love and *who* he's in love with," I asked.

"That's actually a damned good point," Azren said. "I don't know a single god who can mess with someone's mind like that without killing them. I supposed it could be an ability we all have and can master if we're willing to kill enough mortals while we practice.

"Angels were kept isolated in their realm. They were only ever allowed to leave when they were following orders and they had to immediately return home. We never really knew how many angels were created, just that there seemed to be a lot compared to how most gods did their creations. They were also all male, which didn't make sense for the continuation of that race.

"Everything dies. Not even I have the power to grant immortality. Gods have died before. Humans don't have any magic, so their lives are shorter than supernaturals. The gods that created you could have given you more magic and longer lives. You say you want that kind of thing, but trust me, you don't.

"Humans and supernaturals used to live side by side in peace and even now, you fall in love with each other. Outliving anyone is hard and painful. When it's repeated because you were given a lifespan drastically longer than your peers, it's cruel.

"Trust me, the gods didn't give you shorter lifespans because we were being cruel. We have them and it's not great a lot of the time. It's enough to drive someone insane. If they don't go crazy, they get bored and start breaking things. That was done to angels.

"They *can* die because everything does, but I couldn't tell you when that is because no one has reaped one yet. They were created by a god with a massive ego and bully tendencies under some pretty dysfunctional circumstances. Removing him from the equation was just a tiny piece of the puzzle. The fact that they've been alive this long and seen so much of this realm change could have some of them bat-shit crazy and yearning for the past."

"I get what you're saying, but we were in Hell a lot because of Michael and me," Matilda said. "Samael has Lilith, but Lucifer has avoided relationships since his witch wouldn't go to Hell with him. He's one of the most well-adjusted people I know and an amazing extra grandfather to all of us, even if we aren't angels.

"In addition to breaking the rules about how long angels lived, he didn't put any of the fail safes in so that angels got their magic when they turned eighteen. Michael was born with wings and magic. Lucifer has been teaching him since his mind was able to process being taught.

"Michael wasn't always some alpha, avenging angel who threatens anyone who looks at his boyfriend funny and tries to run off his little sister's boyfriends. We're only a year apart and Michael and George had magic. Lucifer would have taught Michael about all of his abilities just in case an angel tried to come for him, but if angels could mess with people's minds, Michael would have totally used it on us. Nothing was sacred for a while."

It wasn't. My mom had the patience of a god because

we were terrible for a while. We accidentally destroyed shit in the house flexing our abilities and came pretty close to maiming an innocent in the carnage. There was a point when things were so bad that if Michael could have mind controlled my twin against me to prove he was stronger than me, he would have. It would have been the worst thing he could have done to me and my dad and I couldn't have fixed it without killing Matilda.

We were thankfully past that now, but my idiot brother liked to pretend he was stronger than me when it came to guys.

"It could be a potion," Oscar said. "We have similar, but they are forbidden and have to be dosed just right. Even if you find the recipe, it's really hard to get the ingredients if you aren't a healer. Potions aren't exclusive to any one race. Angels could have them, too, and easier access to ingredients on their realm."

"Lucifer has been gone thousands of years," Mags said. "When I came back as a familiar, I was surprised at all the new potions that were invented while I was dead and I wasn't dead nearly that long."

"I don't give a shit if it's an angel or a god. They are going after strong witches and that's Mags. Mags is *mine*. I will raze this entire realm if something happens to her,"

"What about your twin?" Church demanded. "George is the strongest witch in this school. She has a massive target on her back."

Matilda gave me a withering glare because my secret was putting Mags at risk. Everyone needed to be focused on Mags, not me. If it was a potion, it wasn't going to work on me. If it was a god, I could use their own powers against them. I *wanted* to tell them, but I kept getting interrupted in some pretty big ways.

I kept the necklace on to hide from any gods who might want to hurt me. I wasn't dating Mags, but I loved her like a sister. If I continued to let everyone think I was a witch, it might bring the killer's attention on me and I could try to stop them.

Or the attention on me could make them go after Mags.

CHURCH

I was trying to control my emotions because we were all about to go talk to Saffron's coven. My emotions were going to leak out and make a shitty situation even worse. Because I was upset and mad as hell. George Bell started as an obsession, but it was so much more than that now. I was still obsessed, but I was pretty sure I was in love with her now.

George was younger than the other two victims and hadn't been asked to do independent study, but that was just a matter of time. She was already being singled out in magical combat and George was fucking brilliant on the dodgeball field. Her family was chaotic and a little crazy, but they were also powerful, intelligent, and had some pretty high-ranking jobs. It was just a matter of time, even though the only time George showed off was on the dodge-ball field.

I didn't want *anyone* else at this college to die, but I needed my girlfriend to worry about *her* safety, too. Matilda and Azren didn't seem to be worried about George, either. Matilda and George shared a womb and Azren had this forbidden romance going on with her. I wasn't a god, but I had opinions about them joining what we had if Azren wasn't going step up and protect her.

But I'd think about that later. If I ever had to have this conversation in my life, I wouldn't want a supernatural in the room who could manipulate emotions and make the whole thing about theirs. Energy vampires were rare, but other supernaturals who could nudge certain emotions weren't.

The moon orgy was officially over. Banshees shrieking would do that. Azren found out what dorm they were in, but we didn't have to ask around for Saffron's coven. A group of men came rushing up as soon as they saw Azren.

"It's Saffron, isn't it? She'd been acting weird and distant lately, but tonight was her anniversary with two of us *and* a full moon. Saffron had finally figured out the recipe for a healing potion she'd been working on that was going to put her on the map. Saffron liked to celebrate in certain ways. She'd never miss a moon orgy."

"It was the same person who hurt Fleur, wasn't it?"

"Is there a place we can talk privately?" Azren asked.

One of the guys was a massive wolf shifter with a ton of amazing tattoos most college students couldn't afford. They were all grieving, but they were mostly angry right now. *My* anger was under control. These men wanted justice. The wolf faced the common room.

"Everyone clear *the fuck* out of the common room. We've got two shifters and a vampire in this coven, so we'll know if you eavesdrop and you do *not* want to fuck with us right now."

"The God of Death also gets cranky when people don't

respect death. Get the fuck out or face divine wrath," Azren purred.

Damn. I'd never been scared of Azren until that very moment. Everyone scurried to their dorms, and we sat across from Saffron's coven. We were all angry for different reasons. I was trying to keep my shit in check and send calming vibes because I didn't want that anger to turn into some kind of mob.

"Yes, it was the same person who hurt Fleur. The board and the Paranormal Investigation Bureau would prefer I lie to all of you and say nothing happened after the Banshees screamed. But this has happened before. It's going to happen again in the present and if I don't stop it now, it's going to be a problem in the future. Were Fleur and Saffron friends? I know they are different years."

"Yeah. All the independent study students are friends, regardless of specialty or race. It's a huge honor to be asked, but not everyone can handle it. It's a ton of extra work and the professors are brutal. You and Professor Morningstar were the only ones who didn't expect them to be geniuses in your classes because they were brilliant in their independent study. They talked about that a lot."

"Yeah, like, all the independent study students are brilliant in their chosen subjects. They're all smart, but they have subjects they struggle in, just like everyone else. Their other professors wouldn't let them mess up. And Headmaster Krauss was the worst about pressuring them to do more than they were already doing."

"She's been bothering Saffron from home. She thinks a witch who hasn't even graduated from college yet is going to come up with a potion to fix the hex she got hit with. Which is fucking ridiculous because her great-aunt was Minerva Krauss. If Minerva Krauss didn't figure that out, shouldn't her family be smart enough to break it when they get stupid and hex the wrong person?"

"Harassing her is more like it," the big, tattooed wolf growled. "She kept threatening to pull her independent study, which would make it hard for any door to open for her in the future...much harder. Saffron wouldn't let us step in and deal with it because Headmaster Krauss is petty enough to expel us."

"She was lying about where she was a lot. Saffron had a fiery temper, and we were constantly fighting about it. We'd just made up and were supposed to put it all aside for the moon orgy. When she didn't show up, we didn't know if she was still mad or that stupid woman pulled her away again."

Wow. The Krauss women were shitty. I didn't think anyone was as bad as Kaylee, but her mom was awful. Was Lindsay Krauss the campus serial killer? She wasn't a strong witch, but George said she stole Minerva's spells once.

"I don't think Lindsay was the reason you thought she was lying to you. I don't even think Saffron knew she was lying," Azren said.

"No offense, but why?" Oscar said. "Headmaster Krauss was terrorizing her. She's plagiarized her great aunt before."

"I'm going to stop you," George said. "Minerva never would have written something dark like that. The blood-lock spell was meant for the Paranormal Investigation Bureau for cases, but she didn't release it because it requires so much blood. Minerva's life mission was to break curses and hexes, not anything that would hurt people."

"Doesn't mean Headmaster Krauss wouldn't," the vampire snarled.

"No," Azren said. "Lindsay didn't do this. She's a weak

witch, and she's not all that smart. She's also worse than carrion birds. Lindsay Krauss is headmaster because of Minerva and a stolen spell. She wants fame, and she knows damn well the only way she's going to do that is by piggybacking off famous graduates."

I wasn't the God of Death or even a scholar. I was just an eighteen-year-old who ran away from home. But I *did* know how dangerously ambitious people worked. I mean, my dad tried to drown me in primary school so I could be a vampire faster and then used me to manipulate people into signing contracts who wouldn't usually go near his business with a ten foot pole. The contracts were always worded that if they tried to get out of it, he'd take them for everything in court.

Azren knew death, but I knew how people like Lindsay Krauss and my dad worked.

"The murders started after Kaylee cursed her and you took over as headmaster. You became a lot of people's favorite professor but a lot of people had some ideas you proved wrong when we found out you're the God of Death. Lindsay Krauss is like my family back in Ireland. She's not going to be happy with secondhand fame.

"Coming back to the Academy of the Profane after getting hexed by a student and heroically catching a serial killer is instant fame. Especially if the killer happens to be the God of Death."

Azren looked dumbstruck for a minute.

"That's…"

"It's plausible," Drake said. "It would also give her an opportunity to get rid of George for good. The two of you were at the scene every time the Paranormal Investigation Bureau arrived. There are a lot of preconceived notions about you."

"No offense, but we all had them," the wolf said. "You dashed them the first day. How are they even going to arrest a fucking god and put them on trial? Even if you let it get that far, she's going to look like a complete fool if they let you get on the stand."

"*If* this is Lindsay, and I don't think it is, I'm pretty sure she's counting on me fleeing back to my realm and not trying to fight it. She disrespected her creator and has been carrying on a petty feud with the daughter of the God of Chaos for years, so framing me for murder wouldn't shock me.

"Lindsay Krauss being able to pull off what I know so far, that *would.* Whoever did this has done it before. And they were bold enough to do it *that* close to Halliwell Square while a massive orgy was going on. That speaks to someone who has gotten away with this enough that they think they'll never get caught and someone with enough power that they think they can handle anyone who comes upon them in the act."

Saffron's coven wanted justice and started chiming in that they were powerful and dangerous, too. I got it. If it were George, I'd probably get myself killed trying to avenge her.

"Listen to me closely," Azren said. "I outrank all of you in terms of power. You aren't going to get better justice than you are from the God of Death. You *can* help me catch the person who did this by getting me in the same room as the independent study students and all their mates before everyone leaves for Yule break."

Tall order considering everyone was going to be leaving in the morning. They said they'd make it happen, and I had no doubt they would. They were pretty fucking motivated. I would be, too.

We had two dead witches and three possible suspects. Of the three, we only had a name for one. Azren might not think it was Headmaster Krauss, especially since she had been housebound since the murders started.

But people like Headmaster Krauss and my dad didn't get their hands dirty when they were doing illegal. I didn't know if there was some secret message board where people like them found criminals to do their bidding, but I stayed with my dad long enough to learn to never let it tie back to you.

Kaylee accidentally hexing her mom had given Lindsay Krauss a hell of an alibi and plenty of time to plot.

GEORGE

Lindsay Krauss hiring someone to brutally murder students and frame Azren was insanely farfetched but also made a lot more sense than an angel or a god murdering college students. I trusted Azren's gut feelings. Unnatural deaths had probably happened on this campus before, but that didn't necessarily mean they were all connected.

Lindsay had a motive I brought up with Azren when we were meeting with the independent study students. Catching a serial killer wouldn't just put her on the map. Azren was a god, so they outranked her. They didn't want the headmaster gig, but Azren did find all the shit she was doing that she wasn't supposed to.

The board was a bunch of greedy fucks. They would have *loved* to keep Azren on as headmaster if Azren could have a revolving door of gods teaching history. The Academy of the Profane was the oldest and best university in the United States, but not the entire world.

They'd been after my dad for ages because none of the other supernatural colleges had a god teaching. Just Azren teaching history put them on the map, but they wanted more. Lindsay struck me as the type to read all the fine print to know which rules or bend and exploit.

She would have known about the cover-up policy when a student died. It wasn't such a huge stretch that Azren was going to break all those rules. Lindsay might not be trying to frame Azren, but her lizard brain could very well be having someone kill students so the board wouldn't ask Azren to replace her.

That was the kind of 'fucked up' we were dealing with. Especially since no one should be able to manipulate memories like that. It was possible with potions if you could get the victim to drink it. It was also possible a god had done trial and error on mortals until they figured out how to mess with their minds without killing them.

In other words, we had nothing.

Azren and I pulled all the independent student students and their mates aside. It wasn't just the witches. We talked to all of them just in case. The board was going to flip, but we let them know they might be a target. We told them to be on the lookout for anyone strange and we told their covens, hives, packs, whatever to come find Azren if someone started acting weird and appeared to be lying. We told them to never go anywhere alone until we found who did this.

It was a start.

I was saying goodbye to everyone as their parents came to get them and take them home. Oscar's abuela and Ren's parents were fawning over me when they realized I knew sign language and I wasn't breaking their duo up. They were both great. Oscar's abuela Rosita said something to

Oscar in Spanish and I laughed because it was funny. She was tiny, and she reached up to tug on Oscar's ear.

"*And* she speaks Spanish. You'd better worship this one and treat her as good as you do your boyfriend."

"Oh, he does."

"She can also read and write Kanji," Ren bragged.

"That's because she's perfect," West said.

I really wasn't. None of the gods were. All my siblings spoke multiple languages because most of our family did and made sure we did. Like, all my cousins were fluent in Old Norse because three of their dads were. My little brother was four years younger than I was and linguistics were kind of his thing. He knew more languages than I did.

Before I could even say anything, someone started shouting. It was loud and someone was angry. When I turned, a well-dressed vampire couple was absolutely berating their child. Belladonna Mortem was red faced and staring at her feet. This clearly wasn't the first time they'd done this, and they felt comfortable doing it in front of the entire student body.

Her parents were *terrible*. I only had three classes with Belladonna, but I knew she was insanely smart and busted her ass, unlike the other legacy students in my classes. As much as I hated to admit it, she was a good co-captain of the cheerleading squad because when she was cheerleading, she took that stick out of her ass, forgot all the vampire superiority crap, and had fun.

Apparently, Belladonna had a perfect grade point average, but her parents were mad that she hadn't been chosen for independent study yet. Which was fucking ridiculous because we'd only just completed our first semester and no one ever got asked this early.

The cheerleading squad was supposed to be a secret,

but they went around talking to her professors and one of them let it slip. Having a dodgeball and cheerleading team at this college for the first time was a historic event, even if we were all terrible and lost every game. We weren't. Both teams were damned good and could win. Her parents were demanding she quit because cheering on lesser races was beneath a vampire.

Church and his grandfather had been standing there with us. They both looked disgusted.

"Some people shouldn't be parents."

"I don't think Belladonna even likes me," Church said. "The only reason she keeps trying to get me in her hive is because her parents want to control that, too. It's why she was only terrible to you once and wasn't even that aggressive about it. Belladonna is ambitious. If she actually wanted me, she'd be fighting you. And unlike Kaylee, she'd be less obvious about it."

Belladonna had been fighting with Matilda much more than she had with me. And the weird thing was, they were on the exact same page with the cheerleading squad and had a lot in common in terms of how they approached classwork. They still fought *all the time, and* I'd never say that to my sister because Belladonna really did say terrible things to her just because she was a Hellhound.

Matilda ranted about her all the time and I think Belladonna would have bothered her less if she had legitimately been terrible at cheerleading, but she was actually damned good.

And for some reason, my twin was storming over to the Mortems taking her earrings off, so some shit was about to go down. I made my way over for backup. My twin could handle two fully-trained vampires, but these people were rich with connections. The rest of this hive was going to flip if she ate these two vampires. I wasn't going over there to protect my sister. For some reason, my sister decided to protect her nemesis and if these vampires tried to get violent, she'd finish it.

These vampires sneered at Matilda like she was total trash, but Matilda never let anyone make her feel anything less than fabulous. She squared her shoulders, braced her feet, and glared back.

"First of all, my twin has the highest GPA out of all the witches. I'm the highest out of the shifters. George's dad is a fucking *god, and* she hasn't been asked to do independent study because *no one* gets asked after one semester. We're still figuring our shit out and the professors need more time to figure out what we're good at. Clearly, the two of *you* didn't have your daughter's insanely high GPA, or you'd be smart enough to know this.

"I'm the co-captain of the cheerleading squad and I'm sorry, but I'm not letting her quit because *you* don't like it. *She* enjoys it and she's good at it. Belladonna and I are going to put this college on the map for cheerleading. Yeah, we are cheering on the dodgeball team, but we are fucking *athletes* and artists. We're dancers and we can win competitions. Besides, she's eighteen and can be a cheerleader if she fucking wants."

"You should mind your business, little girl."

"Sorry, have you met my mom and aunt?" Matilda laughed.

Belladonna finally seemed to have found the spine I was used to seeing around campus.

"I'm not quitting cheerleading. And I'm busting my ass in my classes and that should be good enough for you. My hive is going to be people *I* picked, not people I'm not even remotely attracted to that *you* like."

And then Belladonna grabbed Matilda and kissed the shit out of her. Oh! No wonder she hadn't been coming at me for Church. Church was amazing and anyone would have wanted him. Unless you weren't into guys at all and the only reason you were pretending to be was because your parents were living in the wrong damned century. Humans fucked that up for everyone for a while, but they unfucked it several years before I was born.

All that fighting and ranting and my sister was kissing Belladonna back just as hard. If Matilda had forgiven her for all that terrible shit she said about shifters and Hellhounds, I guess I could, too. If she was kissing my sister like that, *maybe* she didn't believe that nonsense and was just repeating it because it might get back to her parents.

"If you want to make your own decisions and go against your family, then you're on your own. You'll never set foot in our house again until you come to your senses. We'll be contacting the family attorney about your trust fund."

"Then she'll come stay with me at the Library of the Profane over winter break. And I'll be contacting *our* family attorney about her trust fund. Our family attorney is Loki, by the way. He will *destroy* you. Proceed with caution."

Belladonna's parents stormed out and Belladonna looked like she wasn't sure what she just did. She looked equal parts stunned and terrified. I got it, even though my parents were wonderful and supportive. Not only did she just stand up to her parents, but she came out, *and* she kissed a Hellhound. Maybe one day, they'd realize their daughter was more important than their shitty beliefs, but we weren't there yet.

"I hope you know Matilda doesn't unleash our Uncle

Loki on people for just anyone," I said. "Our mom is going to make you apply for a library card, but she does that to everyone and you'll be stuck on the top floor without one."

"Oh, shit. I'm going to pass out. I can't believe I just did that. I've always dreamed about doing it, but they're my *parents* and they've always drilled our family motto into the kids. Some of their beliefs are vile and super outdated, but they're my *family*."

"Breathe," Mags said. "They may be blood, but *real* family loves all your warts and doesn't dictate who you end up with. You might just be joining one of the most accepting families ever. And if you want your trust fund and any hope of your parents being less terrible, you're going to want Loki. He's a pansexual, shapeshifting Trickster who is both a father *and* a mother. He's also a hell of an attorney."

"I never wanted to join your hive, but you're a little more likable now," Church said. "I'm proud of you."

"So am I," his grandfather said. "And I'm going to tell you something. No one in your parent's hive was chosen for independent study while they were students and I know this because I was their headmaster. The fact that they just tore into you in front of all your classmates for not getting picked after one semester when they didn't get picked at all is astounding. I could tell some stories about when they were students. After what I just saw, I'm thinking about it.

Belladonna looked like she was about two seconds from having a panic attack and people were already still staring after that scene her parents' made. Matilda and Mags sprung into action and started steering her toward the front doors so we could walk to the library.

I didn't have being completely wrong about Belladonna

Mortem on my bingo card or that we'd be adopting her over winter break, but I knew my family.

They were going to get utterly ridiculous showing Belladonna what a supportive family looked like. I hoped Belladonna was ready for my family and I hoped her parents were ready for my Uncle Loki.

GEORGE

Yule break was great. I adored my family. The Academy of the Profane was completely empty, so I wasn't constantly worried about someone getting murdered. Our living quarters were much bigger than we needed. The librarian was given the entire top floor of the Library of the Profane and that library was huge. We weren't even remotely cramped with Dexter and Belladonna here.

They fit in great with our family and they made my siblings happy. I already knew I adored the shit out of Dexter, but Belladonna surprised me. Now that she'd dropped all pretenses of trying to impress her family, she was hilarious and I really liked her.

Loki had kind of adopted her since he was going to make sure she got to keep her trust fund. My Uncle Loki knew all about families that didn't accept you. He was born to giants who didn't accept him because he was born to a woman and not created like the other gods. Loki ended up in Asgard with a new family who never really accepted him because he was a Trickster.

Loki *got* Belladonna and my side hurt from laughing any time Loki, Belladonna, and Dexter were in the same room. It ended being Loki who helped me fulfill Dexter's wish to be able to use his wings without worrying about his top. Apparently, back in the day, Thor pissed Loki off. It wasn't even something major. Thor thought he was entitled to something on Loki's plate and Loki intended to eat it.

So, Loki grew Thor's testicles to the size of watermelons and for all the shitting on him they did because he was shady for shapeshifting, no one could put Thor's balls right except Loki. My Uncle Loki had been alive for a while and no one wanted a bored trickster. He'd taken on several different jobs in his long lifetime.

Loki told Dexter and me for a hot minute, he was a pretty 'in demand' plastic surgeon because the theory was the same as Thor's nuts, his work was flawless, and aside from a little discomfort when he was working, it was painless with zero recovery time. He told us how much he loved that job, but some of the people he helped got petty and wanted him to disfigure someone they had a grudge against.

Loki was easily able to walk me through it and Dexter was just so happy once it was done. Now we had two dudes walking around without shirts on showing their wings off. It was less annoying when Dexter did it because my idiot brother always smacked me with his wings and left feathers in my room.

We were coming up on Yule. Everything was decked out in evergreen and there were presents everywhere. My mom liked my guys, but she was going to lose her shit when she saw the painting I commissioned from Oscar. It was *perfect* and better than I imagined.

Two days before we were going to exchange gifts, the shit hit the fan and my living room was suddenly swarming with gods. My aunt was there with her coven and Freya was with them. They all had this look on their face like something was wrong. My aunt and my mom were identical twins, so I knew the look on my aunt's face pretty well.

They summoned everyone because Azren and Drake appeared next. I'd been texting and calling my guys over break. You had to download special apps to call different realms. I had the one to call Hell and Drake and Azren got me the one I needed to call people in the Netherworld.

Freya was holding a huge box that looked like it had been lovingly wrapped. She threw it on the floor like she didn't want to touch it. Freya was beautiful. She was a redhead like Lilith, but a strawberry-blonde with silver eyes like all the gods and a spattering of freckles across her nose. I was more used to seeing her in the body of a tiny, wrinkled witch, but her demeanor was the same. She was pissed and worried about something. Her face was completely different, but I just *knew*.

"I haven't been Freya in a few centuries, but no matter what life I was living, I *never* pissed off anyone enough to send me that."

"Someone better tell us what's in it or I'm going to do that scene from the movie where that really pretty human actor's wife's head is in a box," Balthazar said.

Freya shot him a look.

"Watch it. I'm no longer in the body of a low-powered witch anymore. There are serial killer trophies in that box. Witch hearts. Two are fresh and the rest are much older. Not a lot of people knew I was staying with the Bells. Aside from Azren and the three men I managed to meet every time I was reborn, no one knew my secret until Ravyn's men blurted it out in front of her because of my perfume. Also, I ended up at the Academy of the Profane twice. If the Banshees screamed, we heard about the accident. The academy never pretended like nothing happened. That policy was written after Beatrix died."

"Sorry, but Freya is like my sister," Loki said. "Everyone adored her. We pretended like we hated each other so she didn't get wrapped up in my fuckery back then. I can't think of who would do this."

"I was right about it being a god," Azren said. "And the same person."

Yup. Unless the angels were targeting Freya. It ruled out Lindsay Krauss, and all pointed to a god. Or an angel. Fuck. All we ruled out was my headmaster. All the angels I knew personally drank the powerful women juice and didn't feel threatened. Two of them had to unlearn a lot of brain-washing and my brother was raised to respect women.

The other angels weren't like that. They hated Lilith. Freya never created a supernatural race, but there were a ton out there that left offerings for her in addition to the god who created them. It wasn't just witches.

"It could still be an angel," I pointed out. "We know they don't like witches. Freya has always been an ally, even if no one knows how much. What's more likely? A god made the Academy of the Profane their hunting ground waiting for Freya to show up so they could deliver their creepy gift or an angel is carrying on an old feud and tried to bully Freya, too, by gifting her their creepy trophies."

"I told you she was smart," Freya bragged to Azren.

Belladonna raised her hand.

"Obviously, I'm not a part of this investigation and it's

a little overwhelming being around this many gods, but what if it's not someone who hates her and is trying to bully her? There was this guy at my high school who was obsessed with joining my hive. It was never going to happen. I'm not into guys and my parents wouldn't have allowed it because his family only got rich two generations ago.

"He kept leaving gifts in my locker to impress me. It started with jewelry and the more I turned him down, the more deranged the gifts got. He started leaving dead animals. He got arrested trying to break into my bedroom with a knife and Basilisk potion that would have permanently disfigured me. I don't even know where he got it, but the Paranormal Investigation Bureau takes Basilisk potions seriously. They tried him as an adult and he's serving life. I had to change my number because he kept calling from prison. It could be like that."

My dad huffed. Belladonna's theory was a good one and one I hadn't even considered. She'd clearly been through a lot more than I originally knew. My dad didn't even let anyone comment on her theory. Belladonna was one of us now.

"You're dating our kid, so you're family now. Loki and I can get into his jail cell with no problem. We'll only kill him if you want us to, but we can make his psycho-ass regret ever trying to hurt you and killing harmless animals."

"Ooh, please?" Loki said. "We haven't tagged teamed a fuck boy in *ages.*"

"Um, maybe you should worry about whoever is cutting out my classmate's hearts and delivering them to gods."

"Um, hello? Trickster. I can fuck with that kid, fuck your parents out of your trust fund, and plan how I'm going to thoroughly fuck my wife without even getting a headache."

"You don't have to brag, love," Aunt Ravyn said. "This serial killer takes precedence."

"So, we've got two possible suspects, but no actual names and neither should be able to manipulate memories without serious side effects or killing someone. I need to research," Azren said. "George, Drake, and I came as soon as Freya texted, but we have your Yule gifts back at my place. How'd you like to see the Netherworld? I can get you back before it's time to exchange gifts."

Drake gave me big puppy-dog eyes. Asshole. I really wanted to go, but how was I supposed to say no to that face?

"Pretty please? Our Yule traditions are mostly different, but everyone goes ridiculously overboard. Like, more than your family does."

I was already sold, but we had a ton of holidays that went by the lunar calendar. Everyone went all out. Yule was my mom's favorite holiday, so we had everyone's family traditions, Bram brought some over from Hell, and my dad told my mom about some older traditions that were pretty amazing, but fell out of favor.

"I would have said yes without you fighting dirty, asshole."

"You know you love it," Drake said, blowing a kiss at me.

I was pretty sure the only reason he didn't spank me this time was because my entire family was sitting in my living room. Azren held their arm out and I took it. Azren was my tutor, and we talked all the time. I was crazy about them and wanted things to go further.

One of the quickest ways to get insight into any god was to visit a realm they created, and I was getting a front row seat to the Netherworld.

AZREN

ealms were a lot like mortals who liked browsing real estate listings. Everyone was curious and wanted a peek. Some were these vast, mostly empty places populated exclusively by gods. Others were like mine, where our creations lived and thrived. Most of them had been keyed so that outsiders couldn't get in without a resident bringing them.

Some of that was to keep gods out. Some were to keep everyone out. Mine was completely open, but no one really got curious enough to visit. Probably because none of their locks and precautions could keep me or any of my creations out. They were terrified of us because nothing kept Death out.

George had never been scared of me. I mean, she punched me in the face. She seemed to like kissing me, too, and kept pressing for more. Inviting her to my realm was the god equivalent of meeting the parents. Most of us didn't have parents. Your realm and how your creations lived said a lot about you.

There were only a few gods who didn't think I was a villain and had come here. Freya loved it here. She recovered here every time her witch body died, and she lost her mates. She met the same three mortal men in every lifetime. It was unheard of for an essence to be reborn that fast, but it happened every time Freya went back into a witch.

I was *supposed* to be helping her with that, but then I got that feeling again and she told me to look out for George. That was all I set out to do. That, and catch a killer. But then I fell for her and now I was inviting her back to my realm.

I was older than the universe and I was actually terrified. I'd been in relationships before—with men and women. I wasn't remotely a virgin. I'd had sex as a man and a woman. I knew how to treat my partner.

George was my first relationship with another god, even at my age. I didn't have to worry about breaking her or someone coming for her to get me to abuse my magic. She knew I was the God of Death. I'd never have to agonize about telling her the truth and hoping she didn't judge me for what I was or ask that I kill someone for her.

I could just be myself.

I landed us at Ketura's house. She should meet Drake's mom. When we got back, I sat Drake down so we could talk. All her other boyfriends had figured out we were together. I told Drake about it. Even though I was totally crazy about her, I offered to step aside if Drake had a problem with it.

Drake gave me the most 'Drake' look possible, informed me I was being an idiot, and that it wasn't up to him if the two of us got together. It was up to George. And honestly? He was right.

Ketura's security system would have let her know we were outside. Everyone had a house in my realm. No one was displaced. Ketura had a nice three-bedroom cottage. One bedroom was hers, the other was Drake's, and the third was for her cats. I'd created cats and dogs for my realm because I was partial to them and they made good companions.

Ketura came out covered in flour. She had been baking when we left. Her house was decked out for Yule. We didn't do red and green here. We did silver and blue. Most of the trees in her yard had silver branches, and she had blue lights. She had a giant, inflatable Krampus terrorizing an army of lawn gnomes out front.

"Is this her?" Ketura squealed. "Welcome."

"This is my mom," Drake said.

"Seriously?" George said, pulling her into a hug. "Drake has told us all about you. He said we have you to thank for him being so amazing at dodgeball."

Drake was obsessed with finding out what happened to his birth mom, but Ketura was the only mother he knew. They were close and yeah, Ketura was why Drake was so good at dodgeball. Ketura blushed and held George at arm's length.

"I got flour all over you. I was just about to take the last batch of cookies out of the oven and dinner is ready."

"Ketura makes the best pumpkin spice chocolate chunk cookies and Yule technically lasts all month here, so she made a feast," Drake said.

George let out a sexual moan that went straight to my dick. I wanted to hear her moan like that because of me.

"Pumpkin spice chocolate chunk cookies? That's the best thing I've heard in a while. Your realm smells cleaner than Earth."

Before I could say anything, Ketura's nosy neighbor stuck her nose out the front door. She zeroed right in on George.

"Oh, my. Is that a witch?" she asked.

Ferula was a busybody who used to make a big deal about Drake. She tried to get me to banish a kid because he was playing in his own yard. She didn't like that Drake was an outsider. The rest of my realm adored Drake. Ferula could never make up her mind if she wanted to badmouth Drake or try to seduce me. I couldn't stand her.

"Hi, I'm George."

"She's with us, Ferula. Run along now. She wasn't very nice to Drake," Ketura said to George when she noticed the look she was giving us.

"Oh, then I don't like her, either."

"That's my witch," Drake said, smacking her on the ass.

Ketura and I shared a glance. What was that about? She seemed to like it, but it was very much not Drake. Or maybe it was, and I just hadn't seen him around a girl he was into before. George would have corrected him if she didn't like it. And based on that blush on her cheeks, she did.

Dinner was going to be interesting.

GEORGE

zren's realm was beautiful and Drake's mom was amazing. Azren put a lot of care into their realm. The colors were so different from the realm I grew up in and the stars and moon were bigger and brighter. The greenery wasn't all that green. Back home, we had evergreen branches decorating our place. Ketura had branches all over her living room and they *smelled* similar to evergreen, but they were silver.

Yule was a special holiday for supernaturals. When the humans turned on them, Yule was the only one they didn't have to celebrate in secret because humans had coopted some of the traditions for their own holiday.

But we were like humans in a lot of ways. Some people hated the holidays for legitimate reasons. Having magic didn't guarantee a great childhood or a happy family as an adult. It was common to meet people who hated Yule on Earth.

It didn't seem to be like that in the Netherworld. Ketura

and Azren didn't like her neighbor because she had been terrible to Drake when he was younger, but even the neighbor seemed to have the Yule spirit.

I had a great time meeting Drake's mom. I knew he was hyper focused on trying to figure out who murdered his parents, but he adored Ketura and she was *so* proud of him. I found out everyone in Azren's realm had to reap for five years, then they were free to take whatever job they wanted or continue reaping.

Ketura was on her last year reaping when she found a baby stashed under the sink at a brutal murder scene.

"It was fate," Ketura said. "Drake never made a sound. His parent's ghosts told me where he was and what his name was. His mom said her parents died in a car accident and his dad said his parents were bad people who made their money selling black market Basilisk parts to dark witches. They didn't want Drake near that and wanted me to bring him somewhere they couldn't get custody.

"Drake was an adorable baby. He had that red hair back then, and he was a little chonker. He smiled at me and I was a goner. With his parent's blessing, I took him back to the Netherworld."

"You can't tell my girlfriend I was a fat baby," Drake groaned.

"Pics or it didn't happen," I laughed.

"She's going to whip out all my mortifying baby pictures now and my revenge is going to be epic for asking."

"My parents told some pretty mortifying stories about when we were kids when you met them. My mom also decided to dissuade you of the notion that every witch on our realm was after your toenails by whipping out the Library of the Profane's collection of Basilisk smut."

Azren started giggling.

"I wish I could have taken a photo of your face when Ripley dropped that on you."

"Someone should have told me about that before I got blindsided by a kinky librarian!"

"Well, we thought about it, but a lot of them are more about fetishizing how venomous you are than being accurate. Most of these writers are writing about what they *think* being with a Basilisk is like. None of them have actually been with a Basilisk before. I have, thousands of years ago. You only need to worry about dying if you don't listen when they say stop or you've got some weird kinks that involve eating hair or toenails. Sexual fluids are only venomous if they want them to be."

I had a feeling a lot of that was for me, but it was too late. I'd already been thoroughly fucked by Drake, had no problem with consent, and I wasn't into eating hair and toenails.

"We thought it would upset you," Ketura said. "You kind of ran with the whole hatred of witches thing."

"Yeah, I guess I did."

"Now, you two have presents for her back at Azren's place. You two had better treat this one right."

Ketura knew about Azren and me. I dropped hints, but I hadn't told my parents yet. I wasn't ashamed of Azren, but my dad and Azren went way back and I was worried about ruining their friendship. I needed to do that.

Azren held out their arm.

"I live a few blocks from Ketura. We'll take the long way and walk."

I didn't mind walking. I *could* portal and I did sometimes, but I also enjoyed walking. My dad had taken me hiking at some of his old haunts around the globe and told me stories. Bram had done the same in Hell. It meant a lot I was getting to do the same with Azren and Drake.

Drake pointed out the park he played at when he was a kid. I'll say this for Netherworld playground equipment. It didn't look like it was designed by someone who hated kids. It looked fun, but no one was going to break an arm and no kindergartner was going to burn their ass on that slide in summer because they didn't make it out of material you could fry an egg on.

It was also beautifully landscaped with colorful flowers. There was an area away from the playground equipment where Azren's reapers had brought their dogs. I'd only seen Earth, Hell, and the Netherworld, but they all had dogs.

"Does every realm have dogs?" I asked.

"And cats. People love spoiling their pets. Hades couldn't stand his family, so he made a realm away from them that became part of that lore. He loves dogs so much that he gave them three heads. They are kind of like the pitbulls of your realm. They look threatening, but if you spoil them the way Hades does, they are terrible guard dogs that are more likely to lick an intruder to death than stop them.

"Some of the realms that are just the gods don't. They have the animal totems that are associated with them, but they think they are above cleaning litter boxes, walking dogs, or caring for something like that. I'm a cat person. I have a highly recommended service looking after mine while I'm off realm."

"Azren's cats are *spoiled.*"

"That's where Drake went to high school. He was the best goalie they'd seen in a long time, even before he got his magic."

Drake's high school was something. It was a public

school like the one I graduated from, but it looked like it got a *lot* more funding. I got a great education and had amazing teachers, but the building was old, and sometimes major repairs and been shortcuts with patch jobs.

Drake's high school not only looked like it got proper repairs, but it was beautifully landscaped like the rest of this realm. My high school had trees that had been there for hundreds of years, but this one had flowerbeds that were clearly taken care of.

"It's nicer than the private schools back home."

"That's because we don't have private schools here. Funding schools is a top priority because we want an educated society. We don't have people trying to ruin our public schools because they either have kids there or they will have kids there. A few people have tried, but they don't even remotely have support.

"I don't like running things. You know how much I hate the headmaster gig. I prefer my dusty books, scented candles, and bouncing theories off smart people. I had to run things on this realm for a very long time before I could step back. I'm involved in this realm because I'm a citizen, but not in a God of Death way.

"I haven't had to step in and *be* the God of Death in over a thousand years. Everything you see is because of some really effective reapers have been running the Netherworld. We do politics a little differently here than what you're used to. Our politicians are motivated to better health care, labor laws, and wages for *everyone* because theirs isn't different from the people they were elected to represent. We have more than two political parties and even the ones I'm not all that fond of can't drastically fuck up my realm and pull me away from my books without shooting themselves in the foot. This is my place."

Azren's house was so Azren. It was a two-story, Victorian-style house, but it was painted black. There were large, colorful, stained-glass windows and Azren didn't do lawns. They had a native habitat for butterflies and bees. Azren immediately said hi to their plants. Drake rolled his eyes.

"They've been doing that since we got back. Azren went off realm thousands of years ago to shapeshift and cut up with Loki and when they got back, the person they asked to house-sit killed all their plants and let the cat out. There hasn't been a plant murder or cat escape in thousands of years. The descendants of the original criminal are so far removed that tracing themselves back to him would take serious time and research. Azren replanted the garden and eventually rebuilt the house, but they like to bring up the original crime."

"When I need to take a break from research, gardening is wonderful for relaxing and centering yourself."

I was learning a *lot* about Azren. The inside of their house was just like their office. Dark panels, comfy places to sit, and scented candles and books everywhere. A black cat and an orange cat came running in to twine around their ankles.

"I didn't take you for a pop of color with the cat."

"I always try to have at least one orange one. They are chaos gremlins who love to snuggle. There's one shared brain cell among all orange cats, but I haven't figured if it's one shared brain cell per realm or they are sharing one brain cell among all the realms. My void cat is a perfect princess who is brilliant all the time and has never once had to go to the vet for eating Yule decorations."

"We all adore cats in our house. Mags especially. She had one as a familiar the first time she was alive. They were all terrified when she was shifted, even if we adopted them as kittens. They are shop cats at my grandparent's magic shop now. We could probably get one now that Mags is more of a girlfriend than a familiar and doesn't need to be shifted as often."

"Let's change the subject to your Yule gifts," Drake said. "Azren will talk about their cats all night if we let them."

That was...fucking adorable. I spent hours with Azren in their office after class. They'd been rubbing my back and feet while helping me with my magic and we'd kissed several times, but they were still this massive mystery to me. They taught me to traverse the veil and reap an essence if I was with them and could mimic their magic, but all the little details would come with time.

Azren waved their hand and my gifts appeared. I could have done the same, but I put them in my bag since I was spending the night here. The box from Drake was bigger than the box from Azren, but that didn't really matter. I agonized about Yule gifts for all my guys and had to break out the big guns and get second opinions from Matilda and Mags.

"Open yours first," Drake said, bouncing in his seat like a kid. "Netherworld rules. Guests open first or it's bad luck."

"Same time?" I asked.

Drake gasped like I just kicked his puppy and Azren just chuckled.

"Yule blew up when I brought it over and traditions and lore evolved. It really is considered bad luck for the hosts to open before their guests, not to mention a little rude. Do it for Drake."

Yule was loud at my house. I had a massive family. We all opened presents at the same time and then shouted over each other to show off our presents. It was chaos, and I loved it. But this wasn't my home or even my realm, so I could do things differently.

Zion Skinner had been retired for a while, but he was so fucking famous, his dodgeball jerseys were still popular. Drake had gotten me one that had not only been signed by our entire dodgeball team, he got Zion himself to sign it. Zion Skinner autographed memorabilia was rare because if you asked him for one, he told you to get fucked. The only time he didn't tell someone to get fucked was if a kid asked him and he was rarely available in public to be asked.

I let out this huge shriek.

"How *the shit* did you get Zion to sign this?"

"You and West hero worship him, so I knew I was getting him to sign it when I was getting the rest of the team to. I may have told him it was a Yule gift for you and if he didn't do it, I'd quit the team and tell you and Oscar he ruined your Yule gift so the two of you would quit, too."

"And he didn't shift and eat you?"

"He laughed and said he admired my negotiating skills. Zion said I'm a hell of a goalie and if I don't want to go pro when I graduate, to use them in real life."

"I *knew* he was a softy!"

"I *never* said this, but Zion is terrible with technology and pretty gruff, but he adores teaching at the Academy of the Profane. The board didn't seek him out because they were thinking about forming a dodgeball team. Zion found out there was an opening for a magical-combat professor and fought like hell for the job. The dodgeball team happened after he proved he was qualified to teach magical combat. They don't give that job to shifters often," Azren said.

"He's just a big, cuddly bear," I cooed.

"Never say that to his face. This is from me."

Azren handed me a smaller box. Inside was this gorgeous choker. There was a large garnet surrounded by rose quartz. It was gorgeous and looked really old. They started teaching us crystals in kindergarten. It was mostly coloring pictures and little sing-song rhymes, but crystals were just as important as potions for protection and bringing extra magic to your home.

I looked to Azren because they never did anything without a reason and they always dropped some knowledge on me that had been lost in time.

"Garnet helps with courage and positive thinking and rose quartz is associated with love. Contrary to the stories, Hades and Persephone were deeply in love. He never tricked her into staying. Hades commissioned seven necklaces for Persephone from several realms. This one was made in the Fae realm with Seelie magic. I was helping those two with something and Persephone gave me this one. She said one day, I was going to meet the person I wanted to gift this necklace to. Persephone assured me I'd find my person when I was at my lowest. It took a few thousand years, but here you are."

"Now that we're away from prying eyes at the academy and you can't get fired, you are so doing more than just kissing me after telling me that. Now, it's time for my gifts."

I loved giving presents. Even if it was just something I'd crudely drawn in kindergarten, I loved giving them to people. And I was *terrible* at art. I adored picking out the perfect gift for the right person. I had to go to Hell for Azren's gift and add a little god magic to alter the appearance so it fit in with the rest of their collection.

My family had money. My mom's library job paid extremely well. My dad knew where all the gold was stashed back when people worshipped him. My aunt didn't fight him when he said that was his gold and not a museum's. If Balthazar was asked to consult for the Paranormal Investigation Bureau and the person he was looking into had money, he generally stole some if they were guilty. The trust Minerva left Matilda, and I kicked in as soon as we turned eighteen, so I had a cushion to get me started.

I got Drake top of the line goalie gloves. The gloves were insulated and magically protected because dodgeball was dangerous. The balls the team witch didn't tame didn't really discriminate against players. The field edges were lined with black salt so the balls didn't go wild and take out the spectators, but that wasn't going to stop them for going to Drake.

"Holy shit. Are these what I think they are? I thought you could only buy these if you're on a pro team."

"Well, I have a vested interest in protecting your hands because you're an amazing musician, I want to hear all the new things you compose, and Oscar can experience music again by touching your violin. My parents all taught us different things. Balthazar taught us there are no rules on the internet, just don't be an asshole and if you absolutely need to fuck someone up, do your due diligence and make sure they deserve it."

Drake laughed.

"I get how your family got together. You're all agents of chaos."

"Totally. Azren, open yours next."

Finding a book Azren hadn't read with information they might not know was hard, but not impossible. I transfigured the cover to look like one of their old, dusty books but left the interior the same.

"I don't have this one."

"No one does yet. Lucifer has kept journals since he

defected. No one knows how long angels live, but my freshman year of high school, he found a gray hair and freaked out. He decided he didn't want to die without telling his story. Lucifer has been buried in his journals. He wrote an expose about the early days in Heaven when angels were first created, leading up to when they were tasked with harassing Lilith into destroying her creations and when he defected, to the creation and early days of Hell when he got turned into the human boogeyman.

"He let us read it while he was writing it since we're all big readers. It's pretty eye opening. Lucifer got me an advanced copy to gift to you, but it's not releasing in Hell or my realm for another month."

"You'd definitely better fuck our girlfriend because I've never been able to find a history book you've never read," Drake said.

Azren let out that silky chuckle that was always sexy as fuck.

"It's perfect, George. And it has a lot of information I don't know, but want to. Now, get the fuck out of my house, Drake. I want to show George to my bedroom."

Finally.

GEORGE

Azren used their magic to make themselves at home in their office and staff cottage. They could just wave their hands and put it back when they decided not to teach at the Academy of the Profane anymore. But this was a place they spent a lot of time and was just so Azren.

I didn't know they were obsessed with gardening or cats. Azren's house was just like their office and cottage—dark colors with candles and books everywhere. There were colorful houseplants and a whole jungle gym on the walls for their cats.

But their bedroom? This was an opulent den to do bad things to your partner in. The bed was massive with a hand carved headboard with ravens and cats. Cat's paws and raven wings held back red-silk curtains, and they had this lush black-and-red duvet on the bed.

I'd wanted this since the first time Azren and I kissed, but now that it was happening, my usual nervousness when I had sex with someone for the first time was a million times worse. Azren was a god, so if things got too rough, we could hurt each other. They were also older than the universe and most gods weren't celibate.

So, I needed to be better than every man and woman Azren had ever slept with since the universe was created. No pressure.

"I'm nervous," Azren said.

"Bitch, same. I'm eighteen and haven't been to nearly as many moon orgies as you have. Why the fuck are you nervous? You've done this a *lot* more than I have."

"Not with another god. The primordials experimented after we made the universe and had vessels, but after it became clear what my magic was, most of them kept their distance and the ones who didn't did their experimenting and decided on their preferences. Not *every* god is bisexual. The gods that came later tended to pair up with those that were created with them. Some of them were good friends and it would have made things weird. I haven't been with another god since the universe was a baby."

"Isn't the theory the same whether you're a god, mortal, man, or woman? I'm pretty sure sex worked similarly when Loki shapeshifted into a mare so Freya didn't have to get married and got pregnant with Sleipnir."

Azren gave me that sexy chuckle again.

"Oh, the body parts work the same, but neither of us has to worry about getting too excited and breaking a mortal. When we kissed, I called to have my bedroom reinforced so we don't break it. That bed was hand carved by an amazing artist here five hundred years ago. I'm quite fond of it."

"That bed is amazing. Maybe we should do this on something more replaceable."

Azren ran their long graceful finger along a dresser that also looked like it had been made by some reaper artisan hundreds of years ago. Every candle in their bedroom came to life, and the lights dimmed.

"Why did you ask Oscar to paint your mom's Yule gift instead of just waving your hand and conjuring it?"

"Because Oscar is an amazing artist and most people expect them to work for free now. I'd rather support a living artist than use magic."

"What makes you think I'm any different? We treat artists a little differently here, but almost everything in my house is old and made by one."

I groaned.

"I've never had sex with another god before, but how are we going to do this?"

Azren stepped forward and placed a gentle kiss on my forehead.

"On my amazingly comfortable bed that I had reinforced. I don't know who you think I am, George, but I'm the kind of lover who is going to draw things out as long as possible. I'm not going to throw you around the bedroom and give you a quick, rough fuck. You have your other boyfriends for that. I've been alive a *long* time. I've experimented as a woman, so I know what feels good. You should be less worried about my furniture and more worried if you can handle a god who has read every sex book that has ever been written across multiple realms."

Holy shit.

I grabbed Azren and kissed them.

"I love that you're such a huge nerd."

Azren whirled me around and pressed themselves against my back. They started nibbling on my neck while running their hand up my side.

"I love that you aren't too scared to call Death a nerd and punch me in the face."

"I didn't exactly think punching Death in the face through."

"Shut up, George," Azren growled, pinching my nipple just right. "No magicking your clothes off. I want that beautiful body get revealed to me inch by inch as I remove your clothes."

Holy shit.

Azren slowly peeled my clothes off leaving little kisses and bites as they removed a piece. They unhooked my bra with one hand and then lowered their face to take my nipple in their mouth. I moaned as they sucked and swirled it with their tongue. My thong was the last thing they removed, then they sat back and just stared at me. Azren stared at me like I was the most beautiful thing they'd ever seen.

"So perfect," they sighed.

I reached for them and they kissed my breath away. Somewhere in that kiss, Azren magicked their clothes away. They were lean with a rock star body. I'd seen tattoos peeking out from under their clothes, but I'd never seen them in their entirety. It was a lot of black work and florals. It was gorgeous.

I kissed their chest and all the way down because I was going to blow my beautiful god. *Holy shit.* Azren was the same height as most gods, but not as built. Their dick, though? That was fucking impressive. Azren pulled me to my feet.

"You're a young god, George, but I never want you on your knees in front of me."

"How am I supposed to suck that massive thing then?"

Azren scooped me up and carried me to their bed. They

set me down gently and damn. This bed was insanely comfortable.

"While I'm tasting you," Azren said, winking at me.

We could do that. I pounced and wrapped my hand around their cock. Matilda would disagree with me and I didn't want her looking, but Azren had a beautiful cock. It was long, thick, and perfectly formed.

Azren groaned as I swirled the head with my tongue. They were nipping at my thighs. Azren was teasing me, so I teased them right back. I didn't take them fully into my mouth until they started flicking my clit with their tongue. Azren didn't start out too fast and hard. They took me on this entire ride where they'd gently turn up the volume to a ten where I could barely stand it, then coax me back down.

My parents encouraged us to read and never censored what we read. They trusted us to come to them and talk if we read something we didn't understand or found disturbing. I read enough books to know that delaying an orgasm was supposed to make it more intense when it happened.

Azren was just doing it a little differently. Instead of stopping and making me want to punch them in the face again, they'd just ease off, so I constantly felt good but didn't tip over the edge. I was trying to do the same to Azren. I could tell they were into it because when I backed off a little, their hips would chase my mouth.

I wasn't chasing my orgasm or trying to demand Azren change what they were doing to give me one. I wasn't furiously bobbing my mouth and hand on Azren's cock trying to get them to cum fast, either. I was enjoying the ride, and this felt amazing.

Then, Azren suddenly stopped and shifted their hips to take their cock away from me. I groaned.

"Are you *trying* to get punched in the face again?"

"Is that a kink of yours? Because one of my favorite things about you is that you aren't scared of me, so I'm willing to explore it. I have a collection of old sex toys throughout history in the basement. BDSM has been around for ages. I'd be willing to explore getting spanked by you if that's something you want to try."

"I'll unpack that and your sex basement later. You can't eat me out like that and just *stop.*"

"Well, you were sucking my cock like *that* and I've been thinking about this since you kissed me. I planned for several scenarios that I wanted to do you and thought it was time to move on to the next course," Azren said, nibbling on my ear.

I moaned and started pinching their nipple.

"Tell me all about what you planned to do to me."

"I had a painting removed off that wall right there. I had this one idea where I'd take you against that wall and you'd be completely under my control. I also think you'd look stunning on top of me taking what you want. Or we could do my favorite idea. If we take a little cuddle break, we can do both and sleep in."

I rolled Azren on their back and straddled their waist. Azren's eyes were hooded as they gripped my hips.

"I want both. Then I want to wake up next to you since I know we probably won't be able to do this again when we get back to the Academy of the Profane."

"Maybe once I've had you, I'll have to break all the rules."

I eased Azren inside me and they felt amazing. Azren sat up and cupped my ass while kissing my neck.

"You're a stunning, powerful god and you don't have to hide here. Be a god, George."

My dad initially named me Tempest because of the

storm I caused when I was coming into this world. My chest was pressed against Azren's and they were nibbling on my collarbone. The harder I rode them, the more the wind lashed outside, and the thunder rumbled. I could just let go of some of the control I always held.

My hair tickled my back as I flung my head back and ground myself on Azren's cock. Azren reached their hand up to tangle in my hair and gave it a nice pull right when they gave me a love bite on the neck. Their black smoke surrounded me and it was like a million different hands were caressing me and playing with my hair.

Azren was so teaching me that. Every god portalled differently. Lilith walked out of her door, Loki disappeared in flames, and my dad's signature was a pop of light. Black smoke was Azren's signature move, and they'd clearly experimented with what they could do with it. But *I* portalled in purple smoke and I thought it was just a thing that happened when I didn't want to walk or drive.

It could clearly be used for other things and I wanted my guys to feel what I was feeling when I took my necklace off and told them the truth. While it felt like every inch of my body was being caressed by expensive silk, Azren lowered their head to take my nipple in their mouth.

That slight shift made my clit hit their pelvis just right and made them hit all the right things inside me. Azren let out a little growl when I rode them harder and faster. One little nipple bite and hair pull later and I was gone. Lightning lit up the sky and thunder shook the windows as an intense orgasm hit me.

I felt Azren let go, but the position we were in meant a lot of our bodies were touching. Our arms were wrapped around each other and I just buried my face in their neck and rode out the aftershocks.

"Holy shit," I said when I could talk again.

Azren just held me and stroked my back.

"I agree. You're a god, George. Never let anyone make you feel less than that, even with that necklace on. The only people who matter are the ones who care about you and I care about you a lot. That was amazing."

"You're going to have to show me how you did that with your smoke. And I believe you promised to throw me against the wall next."

AZREN

I had been dying to get George alone where it was just the two of us for hours for months. She could have portalled in and out of my staff cottage on campus or I could have brought her back to the Netherworld before now. I was crazy about her and I needed her to know that, but I hadn't come to the Academy of the Profane to find a mate. I was here to catch a killer.

But all the students had vacated campus, so I didn't have to worry about someone murdering them. I wasn't planning on pulling George away from her family during Yule, but then Freya got that gruesome delivery, and I decided to be selfish. I didn't always need to be the better god, and I'd get her back before her family opened presents.

Our night was perfect. We were up well into the morning wrapped up in each other. I was going to have to call someone to repair the crack in my bedroom wall after we moved from my bed and she let me take control.

I woke up with her in my arms and I knew that was

how I wanted to wake up for the rest of eternity like that. I even slept better than I usually did. I still woke up before she did. Drake had always been an early riser. His circadian rhythm was firmly set on morning person.

I portalled to Ketura's to get Drake so we could spoil her. Ketura made damned sure Drake was domesticated and knew how to cook, clean, and be a partner. I barely needed to step in for that. Drake broke a lot of hearts in high school. He had the whole 'goalie musician' thing going on, but he didn't want anything serious. Drake was pretty clear about that, but people thought they could change his mind.

It was different with George and I could tell it was getting serious for Drake. The fact that he thought she was a witch was pretty miraculous. Her getting through his thick skull that not all witches were evil was even more so because I'd known Drake since he was a baby and I hadn't been able to do that.

"We need to make her proper Netherworld food," Drake said.

"Aside from some fruits and vegetables that only grow here, it's generally the same on her realm."

"And the herbs. If we're going to wake her up for breakfast, you'd better shove coffee in her hand right when her eyes open because she's kinda crabby before she gets caffeine. George likes lattes with two shots of espresso with oat milk. Use the pumpkin spice syrup because George, Matilda, and Mags all go nuts for pumpkin spice. Let's do eggs and savory muffins with the herbed butter you can only get here and the sausage that tastes different because you made animals here a little different. She'll love that."

Yeah, Drake was desperately smitten. Probably just as much as I was. There were only two people across two realms Drake paid enough attention to so that he could make them coffee just how they liked it—Ketura and me. Drake had a ton of friends in the Netherworld and had been hanging with them during Yule break, but he didn't know those kinds of things about them.

"You do the eggs and sausage and I'll do the muffins. You'll have to teach me how to make coffee how she likes it because it's weird eating in the dining hall since none of the other staff do except for lunch."

"Only because I like you and you deserve to be happy. And she's *not* a morning person at all and neither is Matilda. Mags drags them both into the dining hall in the morning. Mags or Mina gets Matilda coffee and one of us gets George's. She's adorable first thing in the morning because she hates everything. One of us gets her coffee, Oscar slips her a doodle, and Ren usually steals something and gifts it to her."

I groaned as I chopped veggies for the muffins.

"He didn't happen to steal some really expensive sneakers from a legacy student, did he? That bear shifter has been harassing me about putting cameras in the dorm rooms so the rest of his shoes don't go missing and then his roommate came to complain because he bought his own camera and stuck it in his dorm. Thankfully, the roommate found it before his girlfriend got naked."

"That tracks," Drake said. "Yeah, that was Ren. Ren's Kitsune likes gifting stolen trinkets, and he only steals from people who are being stupid. That guy was sexually objectifying his friend because she's Japanese and Ren promised he wasn't going to fuck him up for her. He *would* steal his fancy shoes."

I started laughing. I needed to find a way to learn all the little details about these men when we got back to the

Academy of the Profane and let them get to know me. George was mine, but she was theirs, too. I might have cosmic powers and the other gods feared me, but my personality was what it was.

I knew enough about her men to know that I was never going to be as goofy as West or as weirdly obsessed as Church. I loved art, but I was useless at drawing. I'd never be able to brighten her day with doodles. Stealing was Ren's thing. I'd buy her things or conjure them, but I wouldn't be caught dead skulking around campus stealing from students who were annoying me.

"You never told me that. I have no knowledge of who actually stole those sneakers. If they are in anyone's dorm room, you might want to move them because he's demanding I toss everyone's dorm. I'm not, but he's a legacy student. If Daddy

makes a big deal about it, the Paranormal Investigation Bureau will."

"Ren's mind works in mysterious ways. Those shoes were Oscar's size, but he gave them to George, who they won't even remotely fit. He said it was because Oscar would wear them and get tackled by that bear shifter, but Oscar could wear them off campus. George can't wear them at all. Sometimes, he steals earrings, but just one and rarely a matching set. I don't know what she's doing with them, but she doesn't keep the shit he stole in her dorm."

She was disappearing them to her bedroom in the Library of the Profane if I had to guess. That way, no one got in trouble if Ren stole something from the wrong person and the dorms got tossed. I might eventually have to order it and Lindsay Krauss definitely would.

"I'm not sure how I'm supposed to get to know all of them while I'm teaching. I can't have anyone think I'm playing favorites and I can't let anyone suspect George and I are a thing. I have to stay at the Academy of the Profane until the killer is caught and everyone will treat George differently. Not in a good way when it comes to certain people."

They would while she still had her necklace on. When she took it off, no one would blink at her being with me and they probably wouldn't even care I was her professor since we were both gods and she was related to the other two gods that made it public they were on this realm.

They absolutely would have accused her of using her body for better grades and the ones who didn't would be ripping her to shreds because they thought an eighteen-year-old witch wasn't worthy of a primordial. Her mom and aunt dealt with that to some extent, but they were older and had more time to pull off some amazing feats.

Honestly, the board was so desperate for gods and the prestige they'd bring, they'd probably just overlook the rule about students and professors. Everyone would be slapping me on the back for bedding a student, but they wouldn't be congratulating her for landing a god. They'd trash her. I was playing it extra carefully to avoid that since the head-master already had a petty feud.

"They're all cool and they know you're with her. Church and West have supernatural noses. Church waits for her in the common room and zips her to her dorm room using vamp speed so no one else figures it out. Ren also has a shifter nose, and he tells Oscar everything.

"They get why you aren't treating them better than everyone else. Especially since they know about you and me now. You demystified gods a lot in your lectures and they just watched another primordial get super petty with the freshmen mean girls. I don't think you have to worry about them kissing your ass. West is still complaining you made him sniff a dead body. His revenge is going to be epic."

I groaned. I'd been around West long enough to know that was true.

"I didn't realize he was going to get so butthurt about it."

"West is a giant orange cat. Seriously?" Drake said.

I started giggling. That was true. I took the muffins out of the oven and Drake showed me how George liked her coffee. We put it on a tray and when we went in my bedroom, she was adorably sprawled out on my bed with her arm flung over her head.

"Is she drooling?" Drake whispered.

"Welcome to married life. Did Mags say how she wakes the twins up?"

"I'm guessing she wakes George up differently than Matilda. What if she zaps us?"

"Hold the tray."

I really didn't know how cranky she was in the morning but she probably wasn't going to zap us if Mags woke her up every day. Still, she was in an unfamiliar place and might panic. I grabbed the coffee tumbler from Drake and started kissing her cheeks.

"Five more minutes," she groaned. "Is that coffee?"

Her eyes cracked open, and I passed the tumbler over. Drake slid the tray into her lap. She immediately took a sip.

"Oh, wow. The coffee is perfect, and this smells amazing. You two are going to spoil me."

She needed to get used to being spoiled. George was a god. Breakfast in bed was pretty minor.

"Can we talk about the hearts?" Drake asked. "They are clearly symbolic of something."

"Why the Academy of the Profane and independent

study students," George said. "I get that students can be easy hunting, but they went for some of the stronger students."

"Maybe they wanted a challenge," I mused.

"No," Drake said. "Even though she's a freshman, George is the strongest witch at school. If they were targeting strong witches, why didn't they go after George? I'm not wishing that, but she fits the profile."

She did because of the necklace. No one could have known her secret because she was careful. She hadn't made these huge displays of power, but you could feel it coming off of her. I thought it was independent study students, but it was gifted witches. It was too soon for her to be asked to do independent study, but she kind of *was* with me. Following her would have confirmed I was tutoring her. Church did it.

I still didn't know who was doing this or why. I didn't know why they gifted the hearts to Freya. But the big mystery was why they hadn't gone after George when everyone thought she was the strongest witch at the Academy of the Profane.

She was also the only one who could fight back because she very much wasn't a witch.

OSCAR

Yule break was amazing, but we all missed George. We missed Church and Drake, too, but I wasn't dating them. We were back at the Academy of the Profane. George's family was there with her and her dad Bram pulled me aside. I wasn't quite sure why. He was massive and covered in tattoos and piercings.

"So, my wife loved the painting you did for her Yule gift. You probably don't know this, but demon and Hellhound magic lies in runes. Most of us have them tattooed on us. Matilda has several where her ballet and cheerleading uniforms won't show.

"I learned how to pierce and tattoo before my kids were born and run a shop just outside the supernatural market. Gabriel draws for us sometimes. George says you have your heart set on doing magical tattoos. You're an amazing artist and I have a bruja on staff who's looking to take an apprentice. She's a little insane, but everyone at the shop is. Rosita is a fantastic mentor and everyone she's taught has won awards. Their books fill out months in advance. I texted her photos of the painting and the drawings you've been giving George.

"She said if you're willing to do the work, she'll work around your school and dodgeball schedule. We both decided if an apprenticeship is too much on top of all that, we'd let you draw custom flash. Our shop is all custom work, but sometimes we post art we've done for people to get tattooed. We'll pay a commission if someone chooses your design and the apprenticeship will be waiting when you graduate."

Holy shit. That would fix the fact that I refused to ask my family for money, but didn't have a source of income right now. Pro dodgeball teams might come knocking again now that the Academy of the Profane had a team. They probably would, but I had massive amounts of self-respect and may or may not tell them to get fucked.

I loved dodgeball. I was good at it. I'd make enough money to take care of my family and retire comfortably. I'd be able to travel the world. Dodgeball didn't complete my soul like art did. Getting an apprenticeship wasn't easy. Getting one with a bruja who could teach me magical tattooing the way I was created to do, was just lucky. George was lucky.

"School and dodgeball practice are a lot and I still need time for George. I'd *love* to draw custom flash until I graduate and do the apprenticeship then."

"Excellent. Your style is different from the other artists at the shop, so it'll bring us new clients. If someone has an idea for a custom design and you're the better fit, we'll send it to you. This way, when you finally come in to apprentice, you may already have fans of your work. If you can learn to tattoo as well as you draw, by the time you finish your apprenticeship, you should have people willing to fill your books up.

"You're also going to want to start social media accounts with your art. It comes with the territory. We have three artists at the shop and we all have different styles and mentor differently. Rosita has been with me from the beginning and everything we're offering you was her brainchild years ago. She'll send you requests once you have your social media set up."

"Um, thanks."

"I'd better get you back to George. She missed all of you during break and video chat really wasn't the same. I know my kids."

I moved to go back to George when someone caught my attention. There was a woman making her way up to the podium in the auditorium. She was much too solid and didn't move like a ghost, but she looked like she was channeling a Victorian widow in mourning who ran through her haunted house in a gauzy nightgown with the requisite candelabra in her hands.

She was dressed from head to toe in black lace. Even her hands were covered. She had a wide brimmed black hat on with a black veil so no one could see her face. It was pretty extra, even for supernaturals. No one did that anymore and supernatural funerals were more a celebration of that person's life than a big morbid affair.

Everyone stopped to watch because it was fucking weird. The woman in black made her way to the podium as slowly and dramatically as she could. I knew we were about to get a different god teaching history, but I could just tell this wasn't a god. I was tall, but all the gods I'd met towered over me. They also didn't move like they had a giant stick up their ass.

The woman in black took the podium, and it finally made sense. I didn't know what Headmaster Krauss was doing outside a dark bedroom yet. Kaylee wasn't a strong witch, so undoing her hexes and curses shouldn't be too hard, but she'd also gotten on the internet to look up an advanced hex and wasn't paying attention to a damned thing in class, so anything could have gone wrong with the hex she threw.

"It's good to see all of your smiling faces again. While I'm not totally healed, the board and I decided this academy is in desperate need of capable, strong hands again. With a few modifications, I can run this academy again with minimal pain. There are definitely a few things that were done wrong in my absence."

Seriously? Everything had been done right. We got a dodgeball team, cheerleading squad, people got expelled who needed to be gone, and everyone was warned about the killer on campus. This bitch decided to continue.

"I need to clear up some rumors that were started in my absence. No one was murdered on this campus. The idea is ridiculous. Two students approached me that they were having issues with the workload here. I tried to help them, but they weren't suited to the pressures of college. They simply dropped out. There was no drama involved. The issue is closed. No one was murdered."

Oh, damn. She just tried to gaslight the entire Academy of the Profane. Everyone was going to trust the God of Death over anyone else on this subject. Everyone was getting restless and starting to murmur. Fleur and Saffron's covens weren't having it.

"Saffron *hated* you. You were the one stressing her out. Demanded she find a cure for your hex when no one has done that before. She never would have left school and she never would have told you that."

"Fleur wouldn't have left her coven. She loved this school and her independent study. She was handling her class load just fine. She *never* would have left!"

The rest of the student body started to chime in.

"Stop lying to us!"

"It's your job to keep us safe."

"You're going to get us killed!"

Azren came to stand next to us with Loki and Church's grandfather.

"This was *not* my idea. I was against it," Church senior said.

"You could have called and warned me," Azren said.

"Me, too. I got up early for nothing. Think I should turn her into a donkey? I mean, I'm not teaching history anymore. What are they going to do? Fire me?" Loki said, yawning.

"I approve of donkey shenanigans," West said.

"This wasn't supposed to happen. The board vote was tied when I left yesterday. We were *supposed* to meet again and vote. I'm guessing the board president staged a coup and overrode the people who voted no on this. Which means I need to deal with this. If you're going to donkey the headmaster, wait until I leave so I can't say I saw it."

I really liked Church's grandfather. Azren's phone went off, and they looked down.

"Just got the email from the board president. Apparently, they want Loki and me to teach history together and then bring Freya in."

"Oh, yes. Lindsay was making a stink about how Reyson treated her kid. The board *wants* Loki, but they know he's George's uncle and saw that video. The people who were for this wanted you teaching together because they thought you'd be a buffer and they'd still get to say they had three gods teaching here. They are also desperate to backtrack the whole deaths thing."

Azren and Loki started laughing. I hadn't spent that much time with Azren but something told me they could cut up just as much as Loki and Reyson could. Azren just shrugged.

"I hated being headmaster. If they want her back, more power to them. I fixed what I could, but eventually, she's going to massively fuck up. I can protect the students better when I'm not trying to run the place."

And we all needed to look out for George. The campus was mad at Headmaster Krauss because she got up there and tried to lie to us about two campus murders and act like the rest of us weren't in danger. They were booing and catcalling. This was almost as bad as when she tried to cancel the moon orgy. If someone died again, their coven would come for her.

I was guessing Headmaster Krauss was blaming George for all this and anything that would happen in the future because she chose not to protect the students.

SOL

I usually hated the holidays. If I celebrated them with my family when I was younger, I couldn't remember. Celebrating with humans just felt weird because I *knew* I wasn't human and a lot of their holiday traditions were taken from the supernaturals they feared. The thing was, I didn't know what kind of supernatural I was and they didn't really want to celebrate with me, either.

The only reason I looked forward to it this year was that the students would be gone. They usually avoided me or were pretty terrible to me, but I always got lonelier when campus was empty. I was the only person in maintenance who lived in one of the old staff cottages, so when the students were gone, it was just me.

But when the blackouts started and students were dying, I was grateful for the empty campus. No one died, and I had the opportunity to search for clues. If it was me, I had to have left something behind. The Paranormal Investigation Bureau always came sniffing around me, eventually.

I never let them catch me, but it had to be more than just me making everyone around me incredibly uncomfortable.

I never found anything, like usual. I even went through my entire wardrobe. I cleaned so much blood at every scene but never woke up with any of it on my clothes. My wardrobe was limited because I didn't have a ton of money. None of my clothes were missing. I was seven feet tall with muscles and nothing about me said shifter. Someone would complain and I'd be fired if I was skulking through campus naked. I was too big to be inconspicuous.

I was hoping to have *something* that exonerated me before I approached the God of Death with my story. Because honestly, I couldn't say it wasn't me. I'd been avoiding them. If they were anywhere on campus, I didn't let them see me.

But there was another person I was drawn to who might be able to get me an introduction to the pretty Death god in a way that they didn't instantly kill me as soon as I opened my mouth.

It was so stupid. George Bell had only been polite to me when I was dropping off her luggage. She also had the same color eyes as me. It was such a shitty thing to latch onto, but I'd never met anyone with silver eyes like mine before.

And she was nice. Most people weren't. I wasn't going to presume since she was polite to me for ten minutes that it meant anything. I watched her, but I never approached her. I picked flowers and left them in her dorm room when she was in class. She could have thought everyone got them, it was the ghosts, or one of the guys she was dating.

I didn't care if she never knew it was me. Sometimes, she braided the flowers I picked into her hair. She looked beautiful. I needed to get her alone because I didn't know how her guys were going to react to me. I knew she spent a good bit of time with Azren, so hopefully, her word carried weight.

Of course, I could be reading this all wrong. We'd only had one conversation, and it was only a few sentences. Still, I'd been trying to figure out who I was for so long and so many people had died. There were now a lot of gods on campus.

One of them should be able to help, right?

GEORGE

istory with Azren and Loki was something. Kaylee wasn't kicked out for tardiness, even if she wasn't late. Azren usually just pretended like she didn't exist but Loki very much didn't. If Kaylee and Paris thought my dad was bad, they really should have kept their mouths shut around Loki.

My dad actually wanted to be there and my mom probably threatened him not to use magic against students so Headmaster Krauss didn't take it out on me. I'm guessing my Aunt Ravyn told Loki the same, but he pored through the rule book so he knew exactly how to break them.

Kaylee made some shitty comment and Paris egged her on. Azren had this serene look on their face, but I could tell they were irritated. There wasn't as much bite in Kaylee's statement. They said they pulled the whole God of Death card on them and terrorized them. It seemed like she was pushing boundaries and seeing if she could get away with it.

Breaking news at eleven. She didn't.

"Wow, you're really annoying," Loki said, waving his hand. Kaylee and Paris's hair erupted into a rat's nest of tangles. "You may have to shave that off."

Their hands flew to their hair and realized how knotted their hair was. West started giggling.

"I have a detangler that'll fix that, but you aren't lionesses and you've been shit to my girlfriend and friends."

"This is your fault, George!" Kaylee shrieked.

Of course, it was. I hadn't even opened my mouth this entire exchange. I just rolled my eyes. Loki apparently didn't stop there. A roach crawled out of Kaylee's hair and ran across her nose. Kaylee shrieked and knocked over her desk. She and Paris went storming out of the room.

"Anyway," Loki said, yawning.

"Yes, anyway," Azren said. "Keep in mind, folks, we have cosmic power and some of us have less patience than others. I'm Death. You don't want to press me."

Azren was looking right at Kaylee's less-vocal minions, who slunk low in their chairs. Azren got about ten minutes into their lecture when Headmaster Krauss stormed in, followed by Kaylee and Paris with scarves on their heads. Headmaster Krauss looked utterly ridiculous in that getup. She looked like a beekeeper who thought the whole beehive was haunted.

"What's this I hear about magic being used on students?" she demanded.

"Section one, part two of the faculty handbook states magic, force, and vampire bites may be used against students for disciplinary purposes as long as no permanent harm comes to the student. It's supposed to teach them respect and how to fight back. Your crotch dropping was being a little asshole and fucked around and found out." Loki yawned.

"And according to the rest of the staff and a good bit of the student body, she's a little asshole to everyone. She mouthed off to a trickster and paid the price. Might consider what's going to happen when a primordial gets sick of her shit."

"Put their hair back! The rule book says no permanent damage and a healer can't fix that."

"No. You and your daughter have a long-ass history of disrespecting gods and it's time you learn. Loki didn't do any permanent damage. Your daughter doesn't need a healer or a god. She needs a lot of time with detangler and a comb while she thinks about the consequences of her actions. By the way, I could have healed that nasty, painful shit all over your body as soon as you were cursed, but you were literally trying to get an innocent eighteen-year-old you have a petty feud against expelled for it when it was your fucking kid that threw the hex," Azren sneered.

I couldn't see Headmaster Krauss's face under the hat and veil, but I was guessing it still hadn't sunk in yet. Azren also hadn't healed her because she was rude to them.

"I'm your boss! I'll have your jobs if you don't put their hair back and heal me at once!"

"Girl, I don't know whose shrieking is worse—your's or your kid's. Again, no," Loki said. "See, I'm a Trickster. I like to know the lay of the land when I'm going somewhere new. You know, memorize the rule book and find out who's in charge. See, I didn't break a single rule. And there's not a rule forcing us to heal you from your kid's fuckery. You can't control a god, sweetness. Only my wife and husband get to do that. You also don't have the ability to fire us. That's the board, cupcake, and right now, they are salivating about being the only magical university in this realm in history to have not one, but three gods educating students. Go sit with your kid and a comb or I'll fuck your hair up next."

"This isn't over!" she yelled, turning to leave our classroom.

"Oh, the issue is closed," Azren said. "And consider the gods at the Academy of the Profane officially fed up. Control your offspring and learn some respect because we've had millennia to figure out how to use our magic without permanently damaging mortals."

"Toodles, bitches," Loki said, blowing a kiss at their back.

Most of the class started clapping because they were tired of Kaylee running rampant and Headmaster Krauss abusing her position. They hadn't just done that to me. There was one particular student who bore the brunt of that, too, and pixies never forgot.

I saw Dexter tap the screen on his phone, then slip it into his bag. I was pretty sure Dexter was going to capture and post it every time those two ended up humiliated.

Lindsay Krauss was eventually going to fuck up so badly, the board got rid of her. And that little pixie boy she and her daughter tormented was going to get the whole thing on video and make sure everyone saw it.

REN

There were several things I'd come to count on at the Academy of the Profane. One thing had become pretty constant. If you fucked with Dexter, you didn't need to worry about his angel boyfriend. Dexter and his phone were deadly weapons. Everyone already knew what happened in history by the time class ended because Dexter had managed to film it, upload it, and tag the whole school and most of the board before Azren and Loki could even notice his phone was out.

Azren was older than the universe and George was an eighteen-year-old witch. I hadn't been around them together much outside a crime scene, but I kind of got the two of them together. Azren wasn't the biggest god I'd met, and they didn't strike me as the type to use their fists to be scary, but Azren was the god the other gods feared.

Drake filled us in on all that. He said back on Azren's realm, there was a lead-lined bunker only Azren knew the location to that was full of essences. Every group had a concept for those. Some humans called them souls. Some of them even knew what we did—that a cosmic process happened where essences were reborn in a new body with no memories of their previous life.

Drake told us some essences were evil every time they were born and taking people before their time. Azren reaped them, but instead of carrying them to the Aether, they put them in these special jars like a boss. And they'd done that to gods, too. Azren could rip the essence from a misbehaving god and put them in time out.

George and Azren had one thing in common. Azren's power gave them a leg up among the gods. George was a freshman, but she gave off the most power in the whole school. The Krauss women were being terrible to them and they were mostly treating them like annoying flies.

Azren finally snapped. Eventually, George would, too. Because something told me, they might not respect the gods, but they knew they couldn't fight them. They were going to be mad about this and instead of learning from it, they were going to take it out on George.

We were in the dining hall for lunch. Some of the faculty brought their lunch from home and ate in their office, but plenty of them ate in the dining hall with us. George's dad and Azren usually ate together with our potions and Arcane Magic professors. Headmaster Krauss never ate in the dining hall. Sometimes, she was here to make announcements, but she never ate.

Headmaster Krauss had a plate this time and her hat and veil couldn't hide that she was staring right at George. I didn't like it. She was up to something. The dining hall was full of faculty and students. Azren and Loki were here and so was her dad, who was supposed to be a master of the Dark Arts. Her brother would probably go avenging angel if they started shit with her. She could also handle it herself if she decided to fight back. It'd be stupid to try anything, but those two had fewer brain cells than orange cats.

Kaylee was ambling across the dining hall with a mason jar. Witches loved their jars and put all kinds of spell ingredients in them. If they bought jarred sauce because they didn't want to make it from scratch, it became spell-ingredient storage. The liquid in it was green.

Students walking around campus with potions was pretty common. I did it a lot. Some of them were healing potions because they felt a bug coming on. Protection potions were common. Some were for beauty. Like, I walked around campus with a family recipe in my tumbler that was supposed to make my fur super soft and shiny since I always walked around with my ears and tails out.

Kaylee looked like she was going to pass us up, then made this giant show where her potion spilled all over George. George just sat there, but Oscar started shrieking in pain. My eyes immediately snapped to my boyfriend. His flesh was literally melting where the potion had splashed on him and black spider veins were spreading out on his skin.

I remembered what Drake said. This bitch had stolen something of Drake's from his room and made a potion with it. I didn't know why it wasn't doing anything to George, but my boyfriend was in intense amounts of pain.

Drake jumped up and sunk his fangs into Oscar's neck. He'd been talking about that journal Ripley gave him at dinner and all the things he didn't know about his venom. It had healing properties if you brewed the potion right and the journal said if someone close to you betrayed you and stole part of you to kill or disfigure someone, then a Basilisk's body carried antivenom to reverse it.

The black lines on Oscar's skin stopped spreading and disappeared as Drake's antivenom did its thing, but the damage was done and Oscar was still screaming in pain.

"You stole my hair from my brush when you broke into my dorm room and pretended like you were trying to talk me into fucking you at the moon orgy."

"I'm expelling George Bell," Headmaster Krauss announced. "I don't know what kind of dark magic she's using that the potion did nothing to her, but it has no place at the Academy of the Profane."

This bitch right here. I didn't know why the potion had no effect on George either. I was grateful it didn't because Oscar was in a ton of pain. She wasn't blaming Kaylee. She was expelling George for not getting hurt.

Now was the time for George to show everyone she was the strongest witch at this school. Kaylee just *broke the law.* George just sat there and reached for her neck where the necklace she always wore sat.

Fuck me. As soon as the necklace was off and on the table, I found out my girlfriend's big secret. Kaylee and Headmaster Krauss gasped like she slapped them, but George didn't comment. The *first* thing she did as soon as the Academy of the Profane knew she was a god was grab Oscar. A white light glowed from underneath her hand and Oscar's skin knitted together like he was never injured. He sighed and squeezed my hand to let me know it was okay.

But George wasn't done. It drastically darkened outside, a crack of lightning lit the sky, and wind picked up in the dining hall.

"You hurt my boyfriend," she snarled.

"You tried to hurt my twin," Matilda growled.

Matilda's eyes were amber and her canines were elongated. Their dad was on them in an instant. Professor

Morningstar put a hand on each shoulder and gave it a comforting squeeze.

"Breathe. I took care of it."

The Krauss women were about to have a baby god and a Hellhound physically and cosmically whoop their asses. I'd be running, but these two weren't exactly smart.

"She's still expelled," Headmaster Krauss sniffed. "Lying about your race on your admissions form is grounds for expulsion."

"We didn't," Professor Morningstar sneered. "We knew she might want to take her necklace off while she was still in school. The board knows."

And just then, Azren and Loki appeared with the board. Azren swooped in with a vial and made a motion with their hands. The potion on George flew off her face into the vial. They stuck a cork in it and went to wrap their arm around Drake.

Drake was livid. I could only imagine he felt violated. He'd feared this since I met him. Kaylee *stole* part of him to disfigure George and hurt Oscar in the process. West was comforting Oscar with me and signing for him. I didn't know what was going on with Church. He was the first one to know she had a secret. He looked stunned and a little angry that's what it was.

His grandfather pushed his way forward. The board was short one person. There were nine people the last time they were here. There were eight now, and it looked like Church's grandfather was in charge now.

Azren filled them in on what happened because we all saw it. Headmaster Krauss kept trying to interrupt, but Azren must have glued her lips shut like they did Kaylee. That wasn't all. When Azren was finished, our potions professor stepped forward.

"Basilisk potions take weeks to brew. It wasn't done in the lab here or I would have known. It had to have been done at the Krauss home over Yule break. Furthermore, there's not a single student in this college who could pull it off without help. It also gives off a pretty noxious odor in the initial stages. Not only do I think Lindsay knew about the potion, I think she helped make it."

I let my nails grow into claws. That bitch hurt Oscar. She tried to hurt George. She was an adult charged with our care and she tried to disfigure them. I was going to *maim* that bitch. Her dress caught fire, and some asshole put it out. Let her burn.

I felt a hand on my shoulder and realized it was Loki. He shook his head at me. Before I knew it, the Paranormal Investigation Bureau was spilling into the room. Fuck. When Professor Morningstar said he had it handled, he had it *handled.* He sent Azren and Loki to fetch the board and called the Paranormal Investigation Bureau since they broke the law.

Azren passed the vial over.

"I collected the potion off of the victims. Drake says Kaylee broke into his room to steal his genetic materials and claimed it was because she was trying to invite him to the moon orgy. They didn't know George was a god when they threw the potion at her because she had a necklace that made her appear as a witch, but they did hurt Oscar, a very promising Brujo. He's already been healed."

The potions professor didn't even have to say there was no way in fuck Kaylee brewed that potion on her own or that she didn't use the academy potions lab to do it. They snapped into action and dragged Kaylee and Lindsay Krauss off in handcuffs. It was immensely satisfying. She hurt my people. They were both screaming they couldn't do this, and it was all George's fault, but fuck them. Play stupid games, win stupid prizes. They threw Basilisk potion in front of a full dining hall. *Everyone* knew messing with Basilisk parts was a life sentence.

"Anyway," Loki yawned. "Azren doesn't want to be your headmaster. I'm a complete shit choice for it. Freya might do it, but she's got other crap on her mind. Your shitty board passed up an amazing warlock because *you* didn't let him in your little university to be an alumnus. You hired a petty bitch with a vendetta against a child and a history of disrespecting gods. You brought this on yourself. If you have any hope of saving face from this scandal, you'll put my brother-in-law as headmaster where he should have been all year."

"And I warned you about something like this when I refused to vote for her," Church senior said. "I was her headmaster for four years. I'm board president now and I'm calling a vote for Gabriel Morningstar for headmaster."

Church's grandfather was probably a hell of a headmaster. George told us her mom and aunt were terrified of him. He wasn't an energy vampire, and he didn't even use his grandson like Church's dad did to get what he wanted. The old board president abused their position and broke the rules, so he just used decades of scaring college students to make himself board president and get the best choice for headmaster running this school.

"Gabriel Morningstar is one of the best Dark Arts professors in this country. People apply here just to study under him. How will we replace him?"

"By letting him pick someone he's taught. His Dark Arts program is in high demand for various professions. Gabriel has been teaching here for nineteen years. Many people specialized with him from an academic standpoint. He taught them everything he knows and then they continued to study when they graduated. If you ask nicely, I'm sure they'd love to teach here.

"And Gabriel gets final say, not us. He taught and mentored these people, so he knows who is *actually* suited to teach, not someone with a famous name or relative who shouldn't be anywhere near students. That's how we got into this mess where the headmaster and her daughter nearly disfigured two students with a very illegal potion in front of the entire student body."

Oh, man. I *really* liked Church's grandfather. By the time he was done, Professor Morningstar was now Headmaster Morningstar, and I was pretty sure between the two of them, there were going to be some amazing changes at the Academy of the Profane.

I could finally process that my girlfriend was a god. She tried to tell us a few times, but there were some pretty big omens that interrupted her. Oscar looked like he was still processing and Church looked a little angry, but West didn't look the slightest bit surprised.

Now that the secret was out, honestly, West shouldn't have been the only one who figured it out. Her dad was a fucking primordial. We'd met her mom and aunt. They were powerful witches. Power was inherited. If George had ended up a witch, she should have had the same power levels as her mom, but she didn't. She was *much* stronger. We should have guessed.

I wasn't mad. If she kept that from us, there was probably a reason we couldn't understand. I was willing to hear her out because she'd been keeping this secret since she was born. She probably wasn't ready to reveal it to the world yet, but she was forced to. The *first* thing George did wasn't cosmic revenge or even trying to lie about it.

She healed Oscar, so he wasn't in intense pain or had to deal with permanent disfigurement.

George turned to us.

"I'll explain in my dorm room. Ren, did you realize that was you who set her dress on fire? When you gained the power of fire, you got another tail."

I whirled around, even though I knew I couldn't see it. There were many different things that could earn me a tail and unlock a new power. I could, apparently, start fires now. I was definitely *not* going to use that responsibly, but I couldn't even celebrate because this could shatter us.

Everyone agreed to hear her out except Church. He stormed out of the dining hall. We were going to have to talk to him later. Church was stalking her at first because her secret kept him fed. He knew it was a big one and said he'd never force her to tell him. Why was he being a dick when she was forced to reveal it?

Because she had several options to lie and keep her secret. She could have used the contents of Headmaster Morningstar's grimoire, since everyone knew it was full of dark magic. Everyone knew she was with Drake. She could have lied and said Basilisks had super sperm that made her immune to that potion.

Both options meant she couldn't heal Oscar. I was pretty sure Azren only left to get the board because the necklace was off and she could do it now.

I didn't know *why* she decided to pretend she was a witch, but I had a big feeling the reason that the secret was out was because Oscar was seriously hurt.

I was going to make sure everyone in our coven knew that. If they didn't understand she was willing to out herself to protect us, then they didn't deserve to be in our coven.

WEST

Oscar and Ren stayed behind but were going to head to George's dorm soon. We got they needed five minutes. They were together before we ever met George and they needed to talk. I didn't think either of them was going to react badly to George being a god, but they needed to process it together. Oscar just got seriously injured and Ren got fire powers and a new tail.

George wasn't clingy, but I was. I planned to go after Church because he was being a fuckhead, but I needed to check on my lioness. I knew she eventually intended on telling the coven when the time was right, but not the entire school. Dexter documented every time one of the Krausses got dragged, but he adored George. He wouldn't post his video without her permission.

But what happened in the dining hall was pretty major. Other students would have filmed it and uploaded it. It was probably all over the internet now. Some of the news outlets probably picked it up because a headmaster getting arrested for trying to disfigure a freshman was pretty big.

I grabbed George and pulled her into a bear hug.

"Are you okay? I know you weren't ready to take your necklace off."

"I wasn't, but Oscar got hurt. Kaylee is terrible in magical combat. She hits the wrong people all the time. Her hex hit her mom, but if anyone else had been in the hall, she just as well could have hexed a student. If Dexter hadn't been in the hall, Matilda could have gotten hit.

"Lindsay Krauss was going to keep erasing her strikes unless the board forced her hand. She can't hurt me, but she can hurt people near me. I knew Kaylee was going to be arrested for that potion. I wasn't sure if her mom was, too.

"It's not going to be the end of it with them gone. Paris would have taken their place. She's a complete idiot. She only got in here because of her family but she's not going to graduate without a headmaster bending the rules about her grades. She hasn't brewed a successful potion all semester, which is kind of impressive.

"I knew she was going to blame me if they both got arrested because she is going to flunk out without them. Paris would try to take me down with her. She's just as stupid as Kaylee and Lindsay are. Someone else would have gotten hurt again when she was trying to get to me. Now, she knows she can't. And it hurt me when I realized some of that potion got on Oscar. It was worth it because I could heal him while Azren and Loki did what needed to be done. I just wish Church wouldn't have walked away."

"I'm going to find him and have a 'come to Bastet' talk with him. Church isn't allowed to be stupid about this. The only reason any of us knew you had this big secret was because Church was stalking you over it. Church isn't allowed to get obsessed with you because your secret tastes good and make this big deal about never pressuring you to tell him what it is, then be a dick over what the secret is."

"He's allowed to have his own emotions about it, West."

"No, he's not. He's supposed to be smarter than me. He has really good grades at the Academy of the Profane and I barely graduated high school. I figured it out. Everyone at dinner should have figured it out when they met your mom and aunt. I scraped my ass out of every science class in high school with a very low D that I managed at the last minute by using the fact that I'm sexy to get some extra credit. I mostly graduated high school because I'm hot, George. Even *I* know if you got your mom's genes instead of your dad's, you wouldn't be giving off that much more power than your mom."

She nuzzled my neck.

"You aren't allowed to put yourself down when it comes to intelligence, West. High-school grades don't count. You're so smart in other ways. You might think it was obvious, but plenty of people have met my mom and it never crossed their minds. I'm talking about several principals and many high-school teachers who thought I was just an unfortunate witch who got their magic early. They never guessed. Plus, a lot of people can't do what you do with Oscar. I'll go all god mojo on you if you do that again."

"That could be kinky," I said, grabbing her ass. "But I need to go talk to a certain energy vampire to make sure he knows what he's giving up if he wants to be a dick about this."

"He's allowed to be mad, West."

I kissed her and bounded up to our dorm room. Yeah, Church could be as butthurt as he wanted. But after that many moon orgies and crime scenes, he could at least hear her out. He didn't even have to sniff a dead body, but he was there.

Church was pacing when I burst into our dorm room. His hair was a hot mess, like he'd been running his fingers through it.

"I thought I was the only one who was pissed."

"I can't talk for Baby Drake because he stayed behind to talk to Azren. Oscar and Ren are talking and then they are all headed to her dorm to hear her out. I guessed her secret months ago. You're the only one too fuck-headed to even let her explain. Church, you're the one who told us she had a secret. Fuck, man. You *knew* she had one."

"I wasn't expecting her to be lying about who she is!"

"She didn't lie about who she is. She lied about what she is. George is still that girl who laughs too loud and gets nervous before sex because she's worried we aren't going to like it. You met three gods before you knew what she was. They aren't perfect. George is different from them because she's only been alive eighteen years. She had to go to kindergarten and deal with puberty. George is just like us."

In more ways than Church could possibly know, but she needed to be the only one to tell him he could teach her how to be an energy vampire. This wasn't my story. I was just trying to kick Church in the ass so he'd listen.

"But she's not! Why is she even here? There's not even a program for gods here. She can't learn anything. George took a spot from someone who could actually benefit from the program. Did she just feel like slumming it? We aren't her coven because she's not a witch. She's just going to leave us for Azren."

Is that was this was? Church thought George was just messing with us for shits and giggles and was going to fuck off with Azren in the end? I grabbed Church and gave him a very straight kiss on the mouth to get his attention.

"Listen, butthead. She might not be a witch, but she's still a part of Oscar's coven, my pride, and *your* hive. So is Azren. She's happy with that and she knew it when she took up with us. George has never corrected me when I've called her my lioness or part of my pride."

"She still should have told *us* before she told everyone."

I still didn't get how none of them guessed before now. Like, it was pretty fucking obvious.

"She planned on it. Then Oscar got hurt. Just hear her out, man."

"Can I have five minutes to just be upset? I'll hear her out, but I just need to be alone for a bit. And you can't kiss me like that and say you're totally straight."

"Don't take too long. And I didn't use tongue, so it was a totally straight kiss."

I needed to run back to George's dorm. She didn't need me to protect her physically but emotionally was another story.

GEORGE

oly shit. I hadn't really planned how I was going
to take my necklace off, but in my head, I told
the people I cared about before I told the entire
world. Dexter wasn't the only one filming, but he was
the only one who was going to ask me before he posted it. It
was all out there now and since Kaylee and Lindsay decided
to be as stupid as possible and land themselves life
sentences, it was probably viral by now.

My whole life, I'd been worried about what another god
was going to do when the necklace came off. Now, I was
terrified I'd permanently ruined my relationships with
everyone but Azren and West. Oscar got hurt because
Kaylee thought that potion would do something to me. Ren
was probably furious about that. Drake had been paranoid
since I met him over this exact scenario. It was a violation
and the only reason it happened was me. Church had been
all in from the start and now he wouldn't even look at me.

I knew Ren and Oscar needed to talk. West left to follow Church. Azren pulled Drake aside. Matilda did a twin check and as much as I needed her right now, I didn't need my sister fucking up my boyfriends because they didn't like my explanation.

So, I was alone in my dorm room slowly going insane. It had probably only been five minutes since West left, but it felt like an eternity. Lindsay and Kaylee's assets were going to be seized and distributed to everyone that potion harmed and Drake, since they stole his genetic material. Losing all the money and the big house she had from the spell she stole from Minerva and the job plenty of people would kill to have was probably the best revenge anyone could get on those two, but I should have nipped this in the bud ages ago.

Drake was the first person to make it to my dorm room. Drake and I started out rocky, but I loved our relationship now. I desperately didn't want to lose Drake. He was grinning at me, so maybe this wasn't a bad thing.

"Drake, I'm—"

"You don't need to apologize to me about this. I grew up around Azren, remember? I'm not mad you're really a god. I'm kind of pissed I didn't figure it out. I *know* Azren and Loki figured out how to shapeshift into regular, supernatural creatures. Azren told me you're too young to know how to do that and Lilith gave you a necklace. Honestly, thank you for not embarrassing me when I was being a dick to you. It would have been mortifying if I had been causing a scene and you played the god card. Azren probably would have. They've perfected their resting bitch face, but they have limits."

"Don't you want to know why?"

Drake shrugged.

"It won't change anything for me because I'm not mad. It's probably just as good a reason as when Azren did it."

I still wanted to explain, but I had other chances. Ren and Oscar came to my dorm before I could say anything else to Drake. Oscar still looked pale and shaken, but Ren came over and wrapped me in a massive hug.

"Thank you. There were about a dozen ways you could have kept your secret, but you wouldn't have been able to heal Oscar."

"Don't thank me, Ren. Oscar wouldn't have gotten hurt if they knew that potion wouldn't have done anything to me."

"Maybe not," Drake said. "Azren tells me things. All gods have a weakness. It could be anything, but people have found them and killed gods before. It's not that hard to find those stories. They could just as easily hurt us and other people trying to figure out what that is."

"That's dark, man," Oscar said.

"He's not wrong," Ren said. "They aren't operating with a full deck. Everyone knows the consequences of using that kind of potion. She didn't hide and throw it where George and Oscar couldn't identify who did it. Kaylee did it in front of the entire student body and a good bit of the faculty and her mom never told her that was a shitty idea. That's the kind of delusion we are dealing with here."

"Please don't talk about that outside this dorm," I pleaded. "I did this because I didn't want to watch anyone else getting hurt, but I'm going to have a lot of legacy students pissed off at me and acting like it's my fault Lindsay Krauss is in jail. They all got in because of their name, but they have the same amount of strikes and GPA rules as everyone else or they'll get kicked out.

"Their only hope of graduating was a headmaster who

bends the rules. Most of them are going to be nepotism hires at their family companies. They aren't here to find the mates fate wants them to have but to get handfasted with people who should have been business connections. Most of them have trust funds that are contingent on graduating. They are going to be mad at me."

"They aren't as reckless as Kaylee and Lindsay," Drake said.

I had to warn them because it might not just be students after me. I explained the reason behind my necklace and why Lilith gave it to me. I told them I was either related to, or met all the gods still living on this realm and they didn't share that view on born gods, but if one was on campus killing witches, I couldn't say if they'd come for me now.

I also told them Azren helped me figure out what my magic was, so the Academy of the Profane was exactly where I needed to be, but other gods might not like it. They didn't look scared. Drake just yawned and stretched on my bed.

"Then I guess it's a good thing you're fucking the one god they all fear. They can't even team up on you because you can rip their essence out, too."

Oscar and Ren started laughing.

"Or you could use their power against them," Ren laughed. "Does this mean if you're around me, you could have sexy ears and tails?"

"Yeah, but you'd have to teach me because I don't know how. All I really know how to do at this point is witchcraft and some of Azren's magic."

"Awesome! You aren't allowed to have more tails than me until I have all nine."

"My Abuela is going to lose her shit," Oscar said. "All

through Yule break, she kept telling us not to fuck it up with the pretty witch who knew sign language and Spanish. When she finds out she can teach you family magic, she's going to lose it. If you want to learn it."

"Um, yes!"

"Our girlfriend is a geek," Drake said.

I flipped him off with both hands and he blew me a kiss. West came in after that. He picked me up and sat in my desk chair with me in his lap. West kissed the top of my head.

"Church will come around. He just needs five minutes to be stupid."

"We'll talk to him," Oscar said.

"He's allowed to have his feelings," I said.

"I can't imagine being mad your girlfriend is practically invincible," Ren said.

"It's the lying thing," I pointed out.

"If your girlfriend lies about being a god, you find out why," Drake said.

I hoped so. I didn't want to lose Church.

SOL

That was a game changer. I was in the dining hall when everything went down with Lindsay Krauss and her daughter. I never liked that woman. She was rude and sometimes she'd drop things just to make me pick them up. I wasn't going to miss her. I always liked Gabriel Morningstar. He was going to be an amazing headmaster.

And George Bell was a god.

I knew what I had to do. I waited until her boyfriends left and then I knocked on her door. I braced myself because she could totally flip out and hurt me. She peered out curiously and then smiled when she saw me.

"Sol! Come in. I meant to follow up with you, but I got caught up with school and I think you were avoiding me, big guy."

Follow up with me? Was she flirting? A fucking *god?* She'd been arranging the flowers I left her all over her dorm room. Her twin smiled at me, but her girlfriend didn't. I made the girlfriend uncomfortable.

"Follow up with me about what?"

"Because you have the same color eyes as me, you're the same size as my dad, and I can feel you're *supposed* to have magic."

"You aren't a null," her twin's girlfriend said. "They don't feel like you. You make people uncomfortable because it's not like you were born this way. You feel like someone *took* your magic, and no one wants that to happen to them."

"What do my eyes and size have to do with that?"

"Only gods have silver eyes. You're large enough and pretty enough to be one."

"I'm not a god, George."

If I was, there wouldn't be so much I didn't fucking know. I never got sick, but my head wasn't right. Gods weren't blacking out all over the place with no memory of what happened when they came to and leaving behind a trail of bodies. Didn't most people automatically adore them?

"I think you might be related to one. My cousin and I both ended up gods, but sometimes, when gods mix with mortals, their kids don't end up gods. I've never met one, but back when Zeus and the rest of his family were being

rapey shitbags and not giving a shit about birth control, they called their mortal kids demigods.

"I'd have to ask Azren how much of those stories are true and what's legend. Supernatural genetics are *weird*. It might not even be your mom or dad who was the god. My brother had one angel in his family line thousands of years ago and every other person he descended from was a witch or warlock. He still ended up an angel. Azren would know better. If they can't tell by meeting you, they'll figure it out."

That was honestly the most information I'd ever gotten about myself. Our eyes were the exact same shade of silver. I kept my distance, but I'd seen the gods coming in and out of this university. Some of them weren't as built as I was but they had my towering height. A lot of the humans I'd met told me I should submit my measurements to see if I'd beat a record, I was that tall.

But I couldn't accept it, even if everything she said made sense. It explained everything about my physical appearance and why I felt drawn to her. It explained nothing about my blackouts or why I had no memories of my childhood. I knew about demigods, too. They had been celebrated as heroes. I just made everyone uncomfortable.

"I actually need to speak to Azren and I'm hoping you can present this to them in a way that they don't instantly smite me unless they truly get to the bottom of this and need to. I'm trying to help."

She just smiled at me.

"Azren isn't the type to smite first and ask questions later."

So, I told her everything. My long history with the Academy of the Profane that always ended with black-outs, murders, and me fleeing the Academy of the Profane. I admitted I couldn't *remember* killing anyone or having the knowledge to surgically remove a heart, but I couldn't remember *not* doing it, either. I pointed out I never found any evidence who was doing it, but I never woke up with a single drop of blood on me and none of my clothes were ever missing like I got rid of them after the fact.

"I'm not a violent person. The only reason I keep getting a job here is because it feels like something is pulling me. There's never any evidence in my staff cottage that I'm the one doing it, but I also can't remember anything about that night, so I don't *know*."

"I'm not going to lie. You make me feel seriously uncomfortable and I don't think that's your fault. I think Azren can figure out why you are this way. I also think whoever is doing this has been framing you and gaslighting the fuck out of you. They can do things with memories no one should be able to do. Either that, or you're just insane and it's you murdering students and your brain can't handle it. Azren is here to figure out who's been murdering students. You're either a lead or the killer. We need to get you to Azren," Mags said.

"Be nice," Matilda said, swatting at her.

"Seriously. Everyone on campus is probably terrible to him," George said.

"I'll be *nice* when I know he's not butchering gifted witches."

"No, that's fair. I want to help. I want this to stop, even if it ends up being me and I face divine justice for it. Take me to Azren."

I trusted them that Azren wasn't going to kill me before they had the full story. If it was me doing this, then I had it coming.

AZREN

I was furious. I wasn't into tormenting misbehaving mortals like some of my fellow gods. Some of them were assholes and did it because their ass wasn't kissed properly. Loki and Reyson messed with them when they hurt people they loved or dicked over people weaker than them or just because they didn't have enough money. I'd killed mortals for slaughtering people I loved back in the day and I stepped in when an essence kept being reborn bad, but it was never in my nature to do what Loki and Reyson did.

Until now. I wanted to do bad things to Lindsay and Kaylee Krauss and I wanted to drag it out. I couldn't prove Kaylee had her boyfriend assault Dexter, but I had a whole list of things they'd done to that boy. Dexter got his own revenge, but George couldn't get hers right now.

It wasn't the potion they threw at her. Well, yeah, it was. They violated Drake to make it and hurt Oscar, who hadn't done a damned thing to them. George wasn't ready to out herself as a god and she did because of those two.

It was that part that pissed me off. I think everyone that knew her secret would have preferred the necklace come off, but we all wanted it to happen when *she* was ready, so we never said anything to pressure her. I knew why she took it off, too. Kaylee and Lindsay couldn't hurt *her* but they could hurt other people trying to. It was poetic justice it was Lindsay the first time. It could have been anyone the next, and it happened to be Basilisk potion and Oscar the second time.

I wanted to go to her and make sure she was okay, but she needed to do damage control with her other boyfriends. I wasn't worried about Drake. He wasn't mad at her or me for keeping that from him. Drake thought it was hilarious he grew up around me and knew I'd shapeshifted into mortal creatures before and he didn't figure it out.

I didn't know the rest of them as well as I knew Drake. West already figured it out and was already worshipping the ground she walked on even more than he already did. I could only hope the rest of them heard her out and accepted why she hid that part of herself.

Even if she had already had that conversation and things were good, she still didn't need me. I didn't have this massive, fat head that I thought I could transcend a twin bond. Gemini twins at that. She needed Matilda and then she probably needed to talk to her mom. I'd never be able to replace either of those women.

But then, there was a puff of purple smoke and there she was in my cottage. I pulled her into a hug and asked if she was okay. Apparently, what happened in the dining hall was old news. She found someone who could help with our murder investigation. George also mentioned demigods, which wasn't right. When we had mortal children, they never ended up with the silver eyes.

I didn't know *who* had been working in maintenance, where their magic was, or where their memories went, but how had they escaped my notice? I wasn't the type of person who would pretend like they didn't exist because they cleaned up around campus. Everyone was important.

"Relax. He was avoiding you because he thought you'd kill him. I kind of promised him you wouldn't unless you knew for sure it was him butchering witches."

She told me about his blackouts. I could rule him out with one question. He could be the answer to stopping this, but for the life of me, I had no idea what was going on with this man based on what George told me.

"Send him in."

George opened the door and Matilda and Mags entered my dorm room followed by a golden man. I instantly knew him and he could very well be the one doing this. Some gods came back quickly when they died. They told us unlike mortals, they were aware of everything and the infinite blackness of the Aether. Mortals never remembered their deaths, but gods did. Some gods chose to leave their vessels and hang out in the Aether, but the gods who died said it was different because they didn't choose it and there was no option to leave. And they all stewed on their deaths.

Then there were the ones that didn't come back right away. None of us knew what would happen to one of us stuck in the Aether that long reliving our death, but we assumed it would drive someone insane. We knew they'd come back eventually, but we didn't know *how* they'd come back.

So, we spread stories to the mortals. A lot of them had end of the world prophesies attached to them because we thought the world not ending would be easier on the mortals than whatever violence they brought while they were adjusting to life outside the Aether. The man in front of me was attached to Ragnarok.

This one died thousands of years ago. He was beauty, light, and everyone loved him. I knew the god who arranged his death. It hurt the people it was meant to hurt, but if he'd known the god he had murdered was going to stay dead *this* long, he might not have done it.

Shit. I needed to call his father. He was never the same after his death and his dad had the tools to restore his memories if the damned raven would do it without cryptic riddles.

He looked terrified, beaten down, and horribly confused. I got it. I was guessing after a certain point, he just blocked *everything* out in the Aether. He probably had no idea what happened or what he was when he was hurled back into his new vessel. He was surrounded by mortals, so he probably just assumed he was one.

I thought his magic could come back when he remembered who he was. Maybe his name would bring something back.

"Baldur?"

That was definitely Baldur, who my good friend Loki had killed, but he didn't remember a damned thing.

And I didn't know for sure if he was now a serial killer.

AFTERWORD

Thank you for downloading and reading. I hope you enjoyed. I have a very orange 18-year-old cat who was being very orange while I was writing this book, so orange cats ended up making the book and West is very much an orange cat. My cat is not aware he is a senior citizen, so the fuckery abounds.

Stay tuned to find out who the campus murderer is and if it's Sol/Baldur. I pants instead of plot, but I actually know this one.